ROSES AND REVENGE

PORT DANBY COZY MYSTERY #4

LONDON LOVETT

WILD FOX PRESS

ISBN-13: 978-1983903090

ISBN-10: 1983903094

CHAPTER 1

Something wasn't quite right about the school cafeteria. Yes, it was filled with my classmates. Although some of them were faces I'd never seen before. And yes, they were noisy and sharing potato chips and spilling their juice boxes. But the white laminate tables had been replaced with my mom's walnut dining set and instead of benches, the kids were standing and dancing around on antsy feet. And no one was wearing shoes. Strangest thing of all was that I had somehow managed to sit myself next to Francine Thomas. I never sat next to her. As I liked to tell my mom, Francine was the most annoying kid in the world, and she always hogged all the good crayons.

"Hey Lacey, hey Lacey." Now she was trying to talk to me, and she must have been eating a tuna sandwich because her breath smelled just like fish. "Hey Lacey." Her long round finger shot out, and she poked me in the chest. Again and again, she poked me. Apparently, she was still highly annoying. Her face moved closer to mine. When did she grow whiskers? I rubbed my nose as she tickled it. She poked my chest again as she pressed her face really close to mine. But instead of saying my name, a low purr rolled out of her tiny, whisker covered mouth. Another poke but this time something sharp stabbed my skin.

My eyes popped open. Francine's face melted away, and I was staring into the amber eyes of my cat, Nevermore. He was deep in a purring trance as he kneaded my chest with his paws.

"Let me guess, Never. You're hungry?"

My question excited him, causing the cat to get his claw caught in the fabric of my flannel pajamas. I reluctantly pulled my arms out from under the warm covers and unhooked the claw.

I stared up at my cat as he sat comfortably on my chest. "I can't feed you if I can't get out of bed."

Nevermore stood up, stretched his back, sticking his claws in me once again for good measure before leaping off the bed and heading out, tail straight up in victory, to the kitchen.

My radio alarm turned on with a splash of an old disco tune. "Too late," I said to the radio as I shut it off. "The cat beat you to it again. Sure wish you and Nevermore could sync up."

I lowered my feet directly into the slippers I'd placed under the bed the night before. I literally stepped into the fuzzy slippers and out of the fuzzy slippers every day so that in between getting in and out of bed, my feet were swaddled in them. One thing I'd discovered about my first winter in my wonderful new hometown of Port Danby was that it stayed bone-chillingly cold throughout the entire season. There were plenty of sun-filled days, but the coastal air was perpetually glacial.

I wasted not a second of leftover warmth from my bed and wrapped myself quickly in my thick, plush robe. I'd finally figured out the timer on my coffee machine. As the rich aroma of coffee washed over me on my short journey down the hallway, I decided it had been well worth the three hours of poring over the insanely confusing directions.

I stopped at Kingston's six foot tall cage and pulled off the sheet. The artificial darkness kept my crow from belting out heart-stopping, ear drum splitting caws at the first light of dawn. I'd forgotten to cover the cage once or twice and each time I'd woken to a sound that nearly sent me straight up to the ceiling. Most days though, I was the one startling Kingston awake by yanking off the dark cage cover and 'turning on the lights'.

Kingston turned his bleary black gaze up at me with a look that reminded me of a grumpy teenager being woken for school. I reached for the coffee can filled with peanuts I kept stored under his cage, and he perked right up. His long black wings stretched out. He flapped them back and forth to shake out the sleepiness.

I opened the cage and he walked to the exit to grab a peanut from my fingers. But the peanut dropped and Kingston startled and flew back inside the cage as a loud truck roared past the house. It must have been hurtling at fifty miles per hour along Myrtle Place. The only thing past my street, Loveland Terrace, was Maple Hill and the Hawksworth Manor, a dilapidated, deserted mansion that was the site of a horrific family murder at the turn of the last century. The manor was frequently visited by tourists on weekends, but it was Monday and it wasn't open for visitors during the winter weekdays.

I considered it both cool and mildly disturbing that the town's main claim to fame, other than an ivory sand beach and quaint downtown, was the site of a terrible, brutal murder. The crime, which had long since been deemed a murder-suicide perpetrated by a jealous husband, was something that had sparked to life the mystery solving side of my brain. The clues that I'd found did not add up to a murder-suicide, and I was determined to find out what *really* happened up on Maple Hill.

I stooped down and picked up the dropped peanut. Kingston had recuperated from being startled. He edged his way back out. He pinched the nut in his long, sharp beak just as a low thud hit the wood planks on my porch. The unexpected noise caused the crow to startle again, and he dropped the peanut.

We both stared down at it. "You're on your own, Mr. Nerves of Steel."

Another thud drew my attention to the front porch. It was very early for someone to be at my door. I walked to the front window and lifted the curtain. Two more trucks rattled past on Myrtle Place, shaking the pictures on the wall. I lifted the curtain higher to get a better view of the porch. I had a visitor.

Captain, my neighbor's giant, lovable dog, was gnawing a massive rawhide bone on the top step of the porch. I opened the door and stepped out to greet Captain just as his extremely handsome owner walked around the corner of the house.

I instantly reached up to pull down a curly strand of hair that coiled right back up the second I released it. My mop of just out of bed curls instantly took a back seat to the horrifying realization that I was still in my fuzzy bathrobe and slippers.

"Dash, good morning," I chirruped slightly breathless about being caught in my frumpy morning get-up. On the other hand, Dashwood Vanhouten, my tall, broad shouldered neighbor, looked the exact opposite of frumpy. He was his usual glorious self with his dark blond hair contrasting nicely with a blue flannel shirt. And then there was his award winning, breath stealing smile to add to the overall picture and to make me feel extra dowdy.

I smoothed my hands over the plush terry cloth robe, my prized possession when I wasn't standing in front of my dashing neighbor, Dash. "Excuse the way I look," I said quickly. "I overslept. Or at least I gave it a shot. Nevermore did his best to stop my quest."

Dash had one of those smooth laughs, and it flowed off and over the roofs of town like melted butter. "Lacey Pinkerton, you are one person who never has to apologize for her appearance. You're always a sight to see, even dressed in periwinkle blue terry

4

cloth. In fact, I owe the apology." He looked pointedly at Captain, who had worked up a good lathering froth on the rawhide bone. "Lately, he likes to bring his bones over here to eat. I guess he doesn't like my porch because it still smells like new paint."

"That it does," I said. "Although I'm pretty sure the only noses to smell it are Captain's and mine." My hyperosmia, or extreme sense of smell, always told me when someone in the neighborhood was painting a house, or baking a bread, or planting a fragrant bush. It was a talent that was both a blessing and a curse. My super nose had allowed me to help the local detective, James Briggs, solve a few murder cases, but it was also the reason I had to give up my dream of becoming a doctor. The smells in the science labs were too strong, and I found myself doing an embarrassing amount of fainting. Not a promising outlook for a future doctor.

The din of voices and wheels moving on gravel and dirt rumbled down from Maple Hill. "Something seems to be happening up at the manor." I pulled the robe shut tighter and stepped out to get a better look up the hill. Swirls of dust floated up into the morning air before being whisked away in the breeze.

"Yes. I saw a lot of trucks and trailers heading up there. I checked Facebook. Mayor Price posted that there was going to be a photo shoot at Hawksworth Manor. It's for a commercial or a magazine or something. Guess they'll be here all week. That's all I know. Mayor Price tends to ramble on his posts. I got bored after the first few lines and stopped reading."

"At least you're on his friend's list. I have to get all my town updates through Lola or Elsie, and neither of them are very good at filling in key details. I knew that one day had been set aside for work crews to paint lines on Harbor Lane, but no one told me which day. I ended up with a nice ticket and an extra droopy frown from the mayor. Or at least I think it was extra droopy. Since *frown* is the only face he ever shows me, it's hard to judge."

Dash leaned his arm against the porch column. It was one of

those casual, manly poses that made me think he'd make a perfect catalog model. "I don't understand why he dislikes you so much. Especially considering there is nothing at all to dislike." His grin seemed to be extra flirty this morning. Maybe the fuzzy bathrobe had more alluring qualities than I realized.

"Thank you but I don't think there's one particular thing the mayor finds objectionable. He just doesn't like me as a whole, and he has a special loathing for my crow."

"Ah yes, Yolanda told me he keeps pestering the city council to enact some sort of ordinance that bans crows from the downtown area."

"And by crows, he means Kingston. Fortunately, my bird has a fan club around town. Everyone on the council agreed that Kingston should be allowed. He's sort of become the town mascot. And I think having a big black raven as the mascot of a town famous for a murder case makes perfect sense. I feel confident that if Edgar Allen Poe were still alive, he'd visit Port Danby and never want to leave."

A gust of cold air blew across the front yard shaking some of the leftover bits of snow off the juniper shrubs planted around the border of my house.

"I'll let you get inside before you catch cold," Dash said. "I don't have to work today, so I'm off for a quick flight along the coast."

"Great. Have fun." I turned to go inside but spun back around. "Did you say a flight?"

"Yes, a friend of mine is on business in Europe for the month, so he lent me his plane. It's a sweet little two seat Cessna. It's noisy as heck but fun to fly."

"I had no idea you were a pilot." But then, looking at the man, it was hard not to picture him doing all the swashbuckling, daring things required of his type.

"Yep, I've been flying since I was a teen. My dad and I both took flying lessons together. He gave up on the idea, but I got bit by the Snoopy bug."

I laughed. "The Snoopy bug? Do you wear a bright red scarf and goggles?"

"No, but now I'm thinking I should. I can take you on a ride later this week if you're interested."

"Yes!" I covered my mouth. "Jeez, that sounded desperately eager. But yes, I would love to fly along the coast."

"Great. We'll firm up some plans later in the week. I can fly you over your house for an aerial view. Have a good day, neighbor."

"Have a good flight."

CHAPTER 2

*L*ester was outside of his shop, the Coffee Hutch, arranging his brand new counter height tables. He'd transformed the casual sidewalk seating area into a posh coffee pub, complete with tall walnut tables and leather cushioned, extra tall stools.

My shop, Pink's Flowers, was sandwiched between Lester's coffee shop and his twin sister, Elsie's, bakery. Even though they were sixty plus in years, neither of them had grown out of the sibling rivalry stage. And they each had a competitive streak that was a mile long and a mile wide. For months, Lester and Elsie had been upgrading their sidewalk tables and giving away freebies and raffle tickets to lure customers to their respective seating areas. It didn't even matter if the customer bought anything. They just wanted their tables to be filled, thus giving the appearance that their shop was more popular. This latest upgrade must have cost Lester a small fortune.

"The tables look beautiful, Lester," I called as I scooted the sidewalk chalkboard stand advertising my Valentine's specials out from the shadows and into the sunlight.

"Thanks." Lester waved back. A tuft of his white hair fell over his forehead like the white forelock on a horse. He pushed it aside. "I think people will really like them."

"Yes, I think so too."

"Yes, they'll be wonderful until his first customer falls off one of those nose bleed high bar stools and then sues him for his coffee shop," Elsie said sharply from her front door.

"Oh hush, Elsie. You're just trying to stir up trouble." Lester returned to his shop.

Elsie looked at me. "I'm not wrong. Am I wrong?"

I turned the key on my lips. Elsie knew better than to pull me into the table war.

"I am right," she said confidently. "I'm making my February caramel kiss cookies, Pink. Come try one when you have time."

"I smell brown sugar and butter, and I never say no to brown sugar and butter. I'll drop by later."

Kingston normally flew into the shop in a flurry of black feathers, but today, he marched past with his wings glued to his sides like an self-important man with his hands behind his back, coming to inspect things.

"Well, all right then. So we're getting too lazy to flap our wings, huh?"

Ryder, my wonderful shop assistant, noticed Kingston's pedestrian entrance as well. He shook his head as he finished tying a red ribbon around a vase.

I walked to the hook to hang up my scarf and coat. "I'm worried he's starting to forget how to be a bird."

"I don't think you have to worry." Ryder pointed down to Kingston. The crow had marched straight to a pile of sunflower seeds. "I spilled his can of seeds this morning."

"I guess he smelled them when I opened the door and decided

not to waste any energy with flight when his goodies were on the ground." I finished peeling off all the layers of warm clothes and took a deep breath as if I'd just rid myself of a heavy suit of armor.

"What do you think of the Valentine's bouquets?" Ryder asked as he pointed to an array of bouquets on the large tile island, the central workspace and focal point of my very adorable, industrious flower shop.

For some of the women customers, Ryder tended to be a focal point as well. He was a very charming, very helpful and exceptionally talented florist. Ryder was fresh out of college. When he had enough money saved, he would be heading off to study horticulture around the world. But for now, he worked for Pink's Flowers, and I was lucky to have him.

Ryder walked to the first bouquet. It was a pleasant gathering of yellow roses and white daisies bursting from the top of a bright yellow coffee mug. "This is the 'I like chillin' with ya' bouquet. It's a subtle gift for the guy or girl who doesn't want to come on too strong and who wants to make clear that the relationship is still at the chillin' stage."

I nodded once. "Yes, that works. Yellow is perfect for the chillin' stage."

He walked to the next bouquet, a smartly arranged group of pink roses, white lilies and purple chrysanthemums in a glass vase. "This is the 'I think we might have something here' bouquet for the person who doesn't want to say love but who also doesn't want to *not* say love."

I pursed my lips trying to decipher that one for a minute. "I think I understand. And I'd say those are the right flowers for that particular sentiment." I smiled at him. "You really put some thought into this."

His long dark bangs fell in his eyes as he agreed. Lately, he'd taken to wearing a green and white striped knit beanie that worked well with his longish hair. "I wanted to make sure we had every level of arrangement. That way, if someone wanted to give a gift but they didn't want to send the wrong message and screw up the entire day, they'd have choices. Communication is key."

"Said the guy who pretty much only talks through texting and Facebook."

"Good point. But that's when I'm talking to friends. Flowers on Valentine's Day are different."

I straightened the red velvet bow on the last vase. It was filled with the traditional dozen long stem red roses complimented with frilly green fern and dainty white baby's breath. "I take it this is the 'love you, can't get enough of you, be mine forever' bouquet."

He pointed at me. "That's perfect. I couldn't think up a good name for it. Although, it might be too long for the chalkboard."

"They're beautiful, Ryder. The customers will love them." I couldn't hold back a curious grin. "And if you don't mind me asking, which one will you be giving to your new special friend, Cherise?"

"Oh, that's easy. We are still at the chillin' stage. But we're getting closer to the 'I think we have something here' bouquet."

The goat bell clanged and Lola walked inside. "Who has something? What are we talking about?" My best friend Lola, the interminable flirt, had fallen head over heels for Ryder the first second she met him. (She tended to fall head over heels a lot.) But the second he returned the interest, she flipped back to her feet and the crush ended. That was when I concluded that Lola was more interested in the chase than the catch. The addition of Cherise, Ryder's new friend, seemed to be changing the dynamic again. As a former scientist. it was interesting to watch from a purely social science perspective. Not so much from a best friend perspective, especially when Lola was excited or disappointed or heartbroken about some man she'd met.

Lola stopped at the counter and flashed Ryder a well thought out smile. Just a few weeks earlier, she'd bound into the shop barely giving him a glance. Ryder had been plenty hurt by her lack of attention. But today, it seemed, Lola was giving her lashes an extra flutter or two as she grinned at him.

Lola always wore hats. She had an impressive collection, including some unique, stylish finds from her own antique shop. But lately, she'd been pulling on a knitted beanie, similar to Ryder's. She had braided her curly red hair and she'd pulled on one of her signature concert t-shirts, vintage Bon Jovi, over a long sleeved jersey shirt making her look like a teenager. Ryder was twenty-four, a few years younger than Lola, but I was fairly certain her hair and wardrobe choices had to do with the fact that Cherise was only twenty. My friend was trying to erase a few years to compete with the *younger* woman.

"These are pretty," Lola noted about the bouquets as she hopped up on one of the stools.

"Ryder designed them. One for each level of a relationship," I added. I pointed to the mix of pink roses and lilies. "This one is the 'I think we have something here' arrangement. I was just asking which one he'd be giving to Cherise." Sometimes I liked to stoke the fire a smidgen just to wake Lola up. Ryder would have been an ideal boyfriend for her. He was polite and kind and funny. And now it seemed she might have lost out on her opportunity. (Which, of course, was why she was suddenly interested again.)

Ryder's face darkened some, and I was mad at myself for bringing up Cherise. I was being a nosy posy. But my little side note had sparked my friend into action.

Lola hopped up off the stool. "I'm not sure Cherise is right for you. She doesn't seem very adventurous, and you are definitely the adventurous type. I, for one, have adventurer at the top of my must-haves list for a mate."

Ryder laughed. "A mate? It sounds like you're looking for a gorilla. And you've misjudged Cherise. She is very adventurous," he said, with not quite the right amount of enthusiasm.

I'd only met Cherise a few times, but it seemed Lola's assessment was more accurate. She was extremely timid but well put together as if every hair had to always be in place. Her winter scarves were always color coordinated with the rest of her outfit. Even her jewelry and earrings matched the overall look. And there was the ritual she went through to avoid any puddles or snow drifts on the sidewalk. Not to mention that she wouldn't step foot into the shop if Kingston was around.

Ryder pushed his bangs out of his eyes. His jaw jutted forward slightly. "In fact, you've just made me change my mind about Valentine's Day. I was going to give Cherise the 'let's keep chillin' bouquet, but I'm going to step it up and give her the pink roses instead."

"Ooh, very bold of you." She shrugged. "Do what you like," Lola said snippily. "Makes no difference to me."

It seemed I'd sparked more than a little flame with my comment. I wasn't sure whether to pat myself on the back or kick myself in the rear. I decided to step in and change the tone. My social science observations had gone far enough for one morning.

"Ryder, would you mind finishing up the inventory list? We need to start thinking about vases and containers for spring. And spring can't come soon enough. I don't think my feet and hands have been warm for months."

"Sure thing, boss." It seemed Ryder had had enough of the conversation as well. He grabbed the clipboard that held the running inventory tallies and headed across the shop to the potting area where the steel shelving held our supply of floral containers.

I turned back to Lola, who was still watching Ryder walk to the opposite side of the store. My crow, who had more than a little crush on Lola, had finished the spilled seeds. He hopped up to the work island to perch close enough to Lola so that she had no choice but to scratch the back of his head. Kingston had come up with his own unique cooing sound that he released only when Lola was scratching him. I had named it the Lola purr.

"I feed him. I clean his cage. I make sure he has toys and treats and never once have I heard that sound. He's absolutely infatuated with you."

"At least someone is." Lola's mouth turned down. "I hate the entire month of February."

"I'm not expecting any big bouquets either, but you don't see me feeling sorry for myself." I picked up the yellow rose bouquet and carried it to the front window.

Lola followed me. "What sort of a dimwit would give a bouquet of flowers to the owner of a flower shop?"

"True but you're purposely ignoring the real point." I placed the arrangement in the window and went back for the next one. Lola followed me.

I grabbed the vase of pink and white flowers and headed back to the window, with my mopey friend close at my heels. I half expected her to start circling my ankles like Nevermore.

"Well, what's the real point?"

I turned around feeling slightly irritated. "That it's just a silly day that's been designed to boost the economy. People spend money on flowers and chocolate and cards to remind someone that they care about them. It's certainly not a big deal if you have no big plans or if you don't have anyone to exchange Valentines with."

Lola put her hands on her hips. "So, if a big heart-shaped box of chocolate came waltzing in with a cluster of cute balloons that said Pink, Be Mine, Love—" She paused and seemed to be reading my face, deciding whether or not to continue. I was sure my expression was clear, but she was apparently irritated with me too. She flailed her arm around toward the door. "Love, James. Or Love, Dash. Then you wouldn't be doing a little happy dance?"

"Sure I would. I love chocolate."

Lola grunted. "You can be so stubborn sometimes. Anyhow, I've got to get back across the street. My parents sent two big boxes of old attic relics from somewhere on the east coast and I've got to comb through the stuff and price it."

"Have fun with your box of relics," I called as Lola pushed out the door.

CHAPTER 3

*I*t had been a quiet morning and I'd sent Ryder off for an early lunch. He'd skipped breakfast and was feeling the effects of an empty stomach. My legs grew tired from crouching so I sat down on the tile floor to finish organizing the bottom shelves of the work island. Somehow the space, which was too low for convenient use, had become a receptacle for all of our leftover ribbons and tissue. I'd even found a few sprigs of baby's breath that were still fresh enough to use in a bouquet.

The quiet shop and the mindless task of straightening out the remnants of ribbon and tissue gave me time to think. Which wasn't always a good thing. Lola's imagined scenario of my Valentine's Day made me ponder my own sad relationship state. After my whirlwind romance and short engagement to Jacob Georgio, wealthy heir and now president of Georgio's Perfume, had ended in a cracked but not completely broken heart and dimmed hopes of a happy ever after, I'd found fulfillment in my shop, my independence and my new hometown. But I couldn't deny that my heart occasionally yearned for something more.

I was deep in that thought, trying hard to puzzle out whether or not my relationship with Detective James Briggs was anything more than our common interest in solving crimes, when the goat bell rang. I swept off my pants and my mind meandered through the many flirtatious moments with Dash. Like this morning, even with me draped in an unflattering robe.

"Hello?" a voice called, snapping me out of my thoughts. "Pink?"

I shoved the ribbons I had in my lap back into the bottom shelf and pushed to my feet. "Hazel! I certainly didn't expect to see you."

Hazel pulled off her winter beanie, causing her baby fine hair to stand up all over her head. "You mean you didn't know we were in town?" She held out her arms as I circled the island for a big hug. We held each other for a long moment. Dozens of memories came back to me.

Hummingbird. That was the one word that always came to mind when Hazel Bancroft walked into a room. She was a tiny and delicate woman, who darted around the administrative offices of Georgio's Perfume with the energy of a hummingbird. She was technically Jacob's assistant, but that didn't stop her from pitching in a hand to assist anyone who needed it. I was convinced that she had sugar water in her lunch thermos because rather than slow down after lunch, like most normal humans, Hazel would buzz around the floor accomplishing more than the rest of us put together. She could out multi-task even the greatest of multi-taskers. I'd seen Hazel finish a report, arrange donuts and muffins according to various employee food allergies, set up the board room for an important meeting, and post and distribute the meeting agenda during the span of a normal person's coffee break. And she did it all with a smile.

We parted, and I leaned back to look at her. Hazel and I were both plagued by problem hair, only we were at opposite ends of the misbehaved locks spectrum. I'd spent my entire life fighting a natural curl, and Hazel had been vexed since childhood by hair so

17

straight, so void of curl, there wasn't a hair torture implement on the market that could give her so much as a wave. Hazel had stunning blue eyes that were made even more stunning by the large framed glasses she wore, and it seemed she had never lost her obsession with brightly colored sweaters. The pink and green one she was wearing to ward off the morning chill was bright enough to make my eyes water.

"You haven't aged a day," I said.

"And you're still far too nice." Her gaze swept around to the perch in front of the window where Kingston had positioned himself to watch the birds in the trees outside the shop. Slowly, the wild birds that had flown south in the snowy months were making their way back to town. The trees were starting to sprout leaves along thin, spindly branches, inviting their feathered friends back to roost.

"I see you still have Kingston." Hazel walked a few feet closer but not too close. My coworkers at Georgio's Perfume knew I had a pet crow. In fact, Kingston had been my screen saver at work. But few ever met him in person. The few times I hosted coworkers for dinner, I took care to keep Kingston locked in the bedroom. Unlike my Port Danby friends, my city friends would not have warmed up to a crow standing watch over them while they snacked on cocktail peanuts.

"What brings you to Port Danby?" It was a perfectly logical question, but Hazel looked surprised to hear it.

"I would have thought the news would be all over town. We're here for a photo shoot. I knew I should have sent you an email. I just figured Jacob would contact you."

"Wait. Jacob? Photo shoot? You mean—"

"Yep, the gang's all here. Lydia, and her photography crew. Autumn and Jasper are still the faces of Georgio's Perfume." She framed her own face with her hands and forced a camera ready smile. "And Alexander, of course. He's still location scout. In fact, he saw your Instagram pictures of that creepy old mansion and the wonderful lighthouse. He showed them to Jacob. Jacob decided Port Danby would be an excellent location." She added a mom-like eyebrow lift.

"Don't give me that look, Hazel. I've seen it way too often on my mom's face. At least a half dozen times at Christmas. The engagement ended, and I've never looked back. And I'm sure Jacob hasn't either. Didn't you hint in your last email that he was dating Autumn now?"

Hazel nodded dejectedly. "Unfortunately, that seems to be the case." She plastered on a sympathetic expression, complete with head tilt.

"Seriously, Hazel. I have a life here, a wonderful one at that. I rarely ever think about those days with Jacob." Hazel was one of the few people who was genuinely upset when Jacob and I broke up. The end of our relationship prompted me to take a different career path, a path that led me straight to wonderful Port Danby and Pink's Flowers. Hazel and I had kept in touch through email, but those had mostly fallen off with time. Hazel had never married. Even though she was past forty, she was still living in the small back house at her parents' home. She had dated Ruben, the warehouse supervisor, for six months, but something happened that made her break it off and fast. She never let on what it was, which was probably a mistake because it led people to imagine a lot of unsavory reasons for the sudden breakup. But for someone like Hazel, it could have been something as simple as Ruben being impolite to a waiter or a doorman. Hazel took pride in being kind and positive and well-liked by everyone.

I needed a new topic. "How exciting to think that my Instagram pictures made enough of an impact that Alexander chose Port Danby for the photo shoot. The Hawksworth Manor is a little run-down, but it has so much character . . . and history."

"I'll say." Hazel's eyes widened behind her lenses, sending a pulse of nostalgia through me. It felt like old times chatting with her about this and that. "I read some of the articles about the place." She was short but light and she hopped up onto the tall stool like a rabbit. "Horrible stuff went on inside. A man killed his whole family, kids and all. Who says money buys you happiness? It almost always comes with some kind of intrigue or family secrets."

"Yes, and that particular murder case has more secrets than I can count."

Hazel squinted at me. "I'll bet you've been elbow deep in that mystery. I remember your favorite hobby was solving crime mysteries. And I've read a little about some of your exploits in the newspaper, you and that million dollar nose."

I waved off the flattery and changed subjects. "Are you shooting pictures in the house? It's not very safe inside, and the stairs are definitely dangerous."

"Have you been inside?"

"Oh, uh, I did take a quick look once. It ended up in disaster. It was pitch dark, and the doorknob fell off." I thought briefly back to that morning when Dash came to my rescue after I'd gotten stuck inside.

"Didn't you once tell me you were deathly afraid of the dark? I remember when the lights went out in your apartment. You said you nearly burned the building down with candles."

My face warmed. "I'm embarrassed to say I still panic in the dark. But enough about that. So, Lydia is setting up her equipment outside? What about that unsightly chain link fence the city constructed to keep trespassers out of the house?"

Hazel winked. "You mean like over-curious flower shop owners? The mayor allowed us to take down the fence for the shoot." She glanced around the store. "This place is exactly how I pictured it. You always had such a good eye for color and style." She took in a deep whiff of the floral scented air. "And a good nose for fragrance." She rested her arms on the island. "How is that million dollar nose anyhow? Are you putting it to good use here in Port Darcy?"

"Danby."

"Right. What did I say?"

"You said Darcy."

Hazel laughed as she reached into her coat pocket and pulled out a folded piece of paper. "That's because I had Darcy on my mind. More specifically, Mr. Darcy. I picked this up in the bakery next door. Delicious pastries, by the way."

She handed me the flyer.

I unfolded it and spread it out on the counter. "Spend your Valentine's Day with Colin Firth, the real Mr. Darcy, on the terrace in front of the Sugar and Spice Bakery." I read it again in case I'd missed something.

"I'm only sorry I won't still be in town next week. I'd love to eat a pastry with Mr. Darcy," Hazel noted.

I shook my head. "I don't understand. First of all, there is no terrace, only a sidewalk. And I'm sure Elsie would have mentioned this to me. I'll have to ask her about it."

"You're good friends then?"

"Yes, very."

Hazel looked a little forlorn about my emphatic yes. I was probably her closest confidante at Georgio's, and she took it harder than anyone when I announced I was leaving.

I took her hand. "Let's have lunch while you're here." I shook my head "I can't believe Jacob was willing to part with you for so long. What will he do without you?"

Hazel's face scrunched in confusion. "Jacob's here with the rest of us."

The air blew out of me as if someone had clapped me hard on the back. "Jacob's in Port Danby?" My voice cracked from a suddenly dry throat. "Oh, well. I see."

21

Hazel knew me well enough to read my stunned reaction, even beneath my pathetic attempt to hide it.

It was her turn to squeeze my hand. "I need to get back up to the site. Come and see everyone soon."

CHAPTER 4

*R*yder came back from lunch less hungry and less irritated about Lola's morning visit. It wasn't my place to ask, but I could only assume he'd met Cherise on his break. My mind had been preoccupied with the knowledge that my old friends and ex-fiancé were in town shooting pictures for Georgio's Perfume. I'd gotten so little done, I decided a cookie break at Elsie's would do me a world of good. It would also give me a chance to ask Elsie about the Mr. Darcy flyer. After all, if Colin Firth was really going to be eating pastries next door, I was going to need a new dress, at the very least. However, I was fairly certain the original Mr. Darcy was not going to be taking tea in Port Danby anytime soon.

I pulled on just my scarf, deciding I could brave the twenty foot walk to the bakery without getting wrapped in layers. "I'm just going over to try Elsie's caramel kisses, Ryder. I'll bring you back a sample." I swung the fringed end of the sweater around my shoulder.

Ryder's hands were submerged in the utility sink, and he was elbow deep in potting soil. "No problem," he called over his shoulder. "If I'm lucky, the phone won't ring."

Of course, we both knew that Murphy's Law required the phone to ring the second I walked out of the store. But that didn't halt my quest for caramel kisses.

I stepped out to the sidewalk and turned toward the bakery. A surprised breath caught in my throat as Elsie's tables came into view. It wasn't Colin Firth, but it was Detective James Briggs. Briggs was absently eating one of Elsie's cobblestone muffins as he read the newspaper and drank Lester's coffee. The usual dark stubble covered his masculine jaw line, and his slightly ruffled hair moved in the afternoon breeze, curling up ever so nicely on the collar of his black coat. With a little imagination, I could actually visualize him sitting in a nineteenth century frock coat, cravat and top hat, and I liked what I saw.

In truth, I was never disappointed to see James Briggs. Especially after a long stretch of not seeing him. After Briggs rescued me from the clutches of a dangerous, murderous criminal, a villain who was determined to shut me up for good, I'd invited Briggs over for a home-cooked meal. We had an extremely pleasant evening, laughing and talking about anything except murder mysteries. The harrowing incident had brought us closer than ever. For a short time it seemed that we might be moving toward something more than a friendship. But after the nice dinner, Briggs was called to the neighboring town of Chesterton to help take down a gambling ring, and I got on a plane to visit my parents for Christmas. Since then, we'd both been too busy with our jobs to meet up again. Now it felt as if we were back to square one. Something that became painfully obvious during the first few minutes of our awkward greeting.

Briggs stood hastily as I walked into the table area. (Just like a nineteenth century gentleman.) He dropped his last chunk of muffin back onto the paper plate.

"Please, Detective Briggs, don't get up. It's only a sidewalk, after all."

He looked slightly embarrassed, and I felt a nudge of guilt for the remark.

He didn't return to his seat. "Actually, I have to get back to the office. I've stretched out this coffee break long enough."

For a noticeably silent moment, we just stood, gazing at each other, both of us searching for a conversation starter.

"How was your Christmas?" He found his first.

"It was good. My parents were their usual comedic selves. They are altogether adorable and annoying all at once. But I love them. And I particularly love my mom's cooking. I hadn't realized how much I missed it." I patted my stomach. "I think I'm still carrying her banana bread around with me. How about you? I hope you didn't have to work through the entire holiday."

"I had hoped so too. Unfortunately, it didn't work out that way." A crooked smile turned up his mouth. I'd missed seeing it. I wondered briefly if he had missed seeing mine too.

"I'm sorry to hear that. Is the case all wrapped up?"

He combed his hair back with his fingers and pressed his black fedora hat onto his head, pushing the edge of his hair up higher on his collar. "Yes, I'm back full-time, keeping the streets of Port Danby free of mayhem and mischief. I knew I was leaving it in good hands, which eased my mind when I was in Chesterfield."

"Yes, right. Officer Chinmoor had everything well in hand. Aside from a little incident with a parking ticket in front of the town square. That sort of blew up into a scandal, but I think Chinmoor managed to appease all the conflicting parties."

Briggs' full smile made its appearance. It was nearly as charming as his half smile. "I did hear something about the parking ticket fiasco. But, to be honest, I wasn't referring to Chinmoor when I mentioned leaving the town in good hands. I was referring to my occasional detective's assistant. And her highly skilled nose."

I felt the blush starting, but there was nothing I could do to stop it. Or the giddy feeling that followed. "Ah ha, so I have officially earned the title of detective's assistant."

"I think once you've literally put your life on the line, in the name of solving crime, then you are officially an assistant. I'm just glad no one has turned up dead lately. Speaking of people turning up dead—have you gotten any further on solving the Hawksworth murders?"

"No, I've been too busy. But I am planning a trip back to the library to look at the newspaper archives for the town. So, you would agree with me that the true story remains to be solved?" I asked excitedly. My quest for caramel kisses was uncovering lots of pleasantries that had nothing to do with brown sugar and butter.

"Well, if Hawksworth was left-handed, it seems highly unlikely that he would have used his right hand to take his own life. That gun had to have been placed there. And then there was the strange case of Officer Gilly, who noted his confusion with the misplaced pistol but was then quickly transferred off the case. And out of Port Danby as well. I think you're on to something. I look forward to you unraveling the mystery."

"Now I really have to get back to the library."

A van rolled past on Harbor Lane, drawing our attention momentarily to the street.

Alexander, the location scout for the photo shoot, was hanging out the passenger window. "Hey, Lacey! Come visit!"

I waved back.

"Do you know the group of people shooting pictures at the manor?" Briggs asked.

"I do. Only I had no idea they were going to be there. Mayor Price never accepted my friend request, so I'm kind of out of the loop."

Briggs' head shook slightly. "That Harlan Price is a stubborn old mule. I haven't been up to Maple Hill yet. I've been sending Chinmoor up there to make sure ordinances are being followed. I heard it was a perfume company. I didn't realize it was the company you worked for." He stopped there with his comment. He knew through the grapevine and through my own ramblings that I had been temporarily engaged to the heir to a perfume company. But he only had spotty details. I planned to keep it that way.

"I won't keep you, Detective Briggs. I'm heading in to fortify myself with Elsie's cookies before I get back to work. It was nice seeing you again."

He stood for longer than necessary and gazed at me with those wonderful, dark eyes. "It was nice seeing you too, Miss Pinkerton."

CHAPTER 5

*E*lsie's bakery was a delight for the eyes, the nose and the taste buds. There were always mounds of yummy treats piled high beneath the curved glass on the teal colored counter. And with Valentine's Day just a week away, my friend Elsie had been working overtime creating sweets for sweethearts. Pink and red glistening frosting heaped on plump cupcakes, sugar cookies shaped like Xs and Os for hugs and kisses, and chocolate dipped marshmallows were lined in a perfectly decadent array along the top shelf. She'd even created mini multi-tiered cakes, each with its own glittering design of fondant and buttercream.

Elsie came out from the storeroom with a stack of flattened pastry boxes. Elsie was an amazing woman with boundless energy. But today there were grayish circles beneath her eyes. She had tried to hire some help for the bakery. It seemed she'd found the right person with Sandra, a fresh out of high school young woman, who had aspirations to become a pastry chef. But Elsie was just too hard on her, and Sandra eventually left in a tearful fit.

"Pink, I didn't hear you come in. My head has been in the clouds today." She walked straight to her back counter and grabbed a tray of cookies that were pinched like candy kisses. The bottoms of the cookies were coated in caramel and chopped pecans.

She glanced past me out the front windows of the bakery as she lowered the tray to the counter. "Detective Briggs was outside eating a muffin. Did you happen to see him?" I knew she wasn't asking just to make small talk. She had spent no small amount of time inventing a romantic relationship between Briggs and me, even though it only existed in her imagination.

"We talked briefly," I said coolly, as if I hadn't temporarily lost my breath at the sight of him.

Elsie placed two cookies on a paper plate and handed it to me. "Oh?" She managed to stretch that one syllable into one big, curious question.

"We mostly talked about the Hawksworth murders and the photo shoot up at the manor."

The frilly straps of her apron deflated as her shoulders drooped. "I see. You do spend a lot of time thinking about that horrible murder-suicide."

"It interests me." I took a bite of the caramel kiss. The cookie was a light, delicate brown sugar shortbread robed in rich, buttery caramel. Tidbits of pecans were strewn throughout, giving a nice salty crunch to the sweet cookie. "Genius again, my friend. So delicious. I'll take the second one to Ryder." I finished the cookie and used my finger to pick up the crumbs left on the plate. "Yum. There was something I wanted to ask you about, Elsie." My gaze swept along the glass counter to Elsie's cash register. A pile of the Mr. Darcy flyers sat next to the tip jar.

I walked over and picked one up. "Have you been holding out on me? You know Colin Firth and you actually talked him into having treats with a flurry of admirers on Valentine's Day right out here on the—" I cleared my throat. "On the terrace, otherwise known as the downtown sidewalk."

Elsie's lips pulled in, which meant she was about to confess something. "Well, if you're going to take the flyer literally . . ."

"I won't because I knew if Colin Firth was your friend you would have told me at least a dozen times by now. However, I'm fairly certain that other people will take it quite literally. A friend of mine, who is in Port Danby for the photo shoot, was already lamenting that she'd be missing her Valentine's date with Mr. Darcy because she will no longer be in town."

"Oh, so that crew at the manor *are* your friends from the city. I knew it. I saw the name Georgio's Perfume on Mayor Price's post. I tapped my chin a hundred times trying to recall whether or not that was the name of the company you worked for. Is *he* here too? The ex-boss, ex-fiancé?"

"Wow, that was the fastest change of topic I have ever experienced. My head is still spinning. Yes, it is the company I worked for, and I've heard that Jacob is in town. But I haven't seen him." I lifted the flyer and tapped it with my free hand. "Back to this. Elsie, you can't use this. It's false advertising. You're going to have a line all the way down to the coast and back up along Culpepper Road, adoring fans skipping their real Valentine's dates to have tea with Colin Firth, aka Mr. Darcy. I know Lester invested in some highly impractical but very inviting tables and chairs, but you can't let that—"

Elsie put up her hand to stop my lecture. "It's not false advertising. Mr. Darcy will be joining my customers on Valentine's Day." She opened the swinging gate at the end of her counter and invited me through. Her storeroom smelled heavily of sugar, molasses and vanilla, and it made me slightly dizzy.

Elsie swung open the utility closet door at the back of the storeroom and disappeared inside for a second. She emerged with a six foot tall cardboard cutout of, none other than, Colin Firth, in his youth, playing the part of Mr. Darcy.

Elsie proudly held the cardboard cutout in front of her. "Ta da!"

I blinked at it, a tad too dumbfounded to speak.

Elsie poked her face around Mr. Darcy's shoulder. "What do you think?"

"I think if you don't make it clear on the flyer that Mr. Darcy is one dimensional and cardboard, then you're going to have a lot of angry customers."

Elsie waved her hand past Mr. Darcy's face. "Nonsense. They can't possibly think the actual man will be here. He's a big movie star." She carried the cardboard man back into the closet and shut the door.

I stared at her, trying to work up a response that would let her see reason, but I could tell by the rounded cheeks and firm set of her chin, she was sure all would go well. I was far from convinced.

The bell on the bakery door rang. "Oops, I have a customer."

I followed Elsie out. Lola was helping herself to Ryder's caramel kiss. She licked the caramel off her finger. "Hmm so good. Just what I needed after combing through dusty, mildew rotted *treasures* from the past. By the way, Pink, when you have time, come look at some of the pictures I found in an old keepsake box. I think you'll be interested."

"I will but for now I've got to get back to work. Elsie, if you wouldn't mind, could I get a sample cookie for Ryder?" Just the mention of his name made Lola roll her eyes. I was about to ask her what the eye roll was for and then thought better of it. I forgot that Lola didn't need to be prodded to speak her mind.

"Honestly, Ryder has no idea what he's getting into with that simpering, prissy little Cherise," Lola said in her perfect impression of a jealous sixteen-year-old.

Elsie shot me a secret, all-knowing look as she handed me the cookie.

31

"I don't know why you care, Lola. Just this morning you told him that what he did made no difference to you."

"And it doesn't. Never mind that. What are you wearing next Tuesday?" Lola asked, quickly turning the conversation away from Ryder.

"Next Tuesday?" I asked.

"Yes, when Mr. Darcy comes to share cupcakes with all of us."

This time it was my turn to cast a secret 'told you so' look at Elsie.

I waited for Elsie to clear up the mess, but she stayed silent.

"Elsie, may I tell her about the Mr. Darcy in the closet?"

Lola's mouth dropped open wide enough to fit in an entire cupcake, layer frosting and all. "Do you mean that Mr. Darcy is —you know—?"

"No. He's not in the metaphorical closet. He's in the literal closet. Elsie's utility closet, to be exact."

Elsie finally took pity on a very befuddled Lola. "Oh, Lola, you can't possibly think that the real Colin Firth is coming to Port Danby to eat cupcakes," Elsie said with exasperation. "I found this marvelous, life-sized cardboard cutout of Mr. Darcy on Ebay and I bought it for Valentine's Day."

Lola shifted her eyes toward me without moving her head. "She's joking, right?"

I shook my head. "Nope, I've seen it. And yes, it is marvelous and life-sized. And it's definitely cardboard."

Lola's posture crumpled with disappointment. "And here I thought my Valentine's Day had been saved from being the most depressing day of the year."

I shot Elsie a second 'told you so' look. It might have been overkill. Elsie's expression soured, and she brusquely handed me a cookie for Ryder.

"You two girls might have all kinds of time to worry about silly holidays, but I've got a bakery to run."

Lola was confused again as we walked out of the store together. "She seems mad," she muttered under her breath. "Shouldn't I be the one who is mad?" she asked louder as the bakery door shut behind us. "I'm the one who has been floating around this morning picturing myself twirling around in my cotton muslin dress like a Regency coquette sighing dreamily as Mr. Darcy nibbled his scones. "

I walked with her to the edge of the sidewalk. "I'm worried this is going to backfire badly for her. I'll have to go back later and apologize for being so unpleasant about it. I'll drop by to look at those pictures when I get a chance."

"Yes, I'm curious to hear your opinion."

"My opinion?"

"You'll see," Lola said with a teasing smile.

CHAPTER 6

*K*ingston came in from his afternoon tour of the town looking lonely and dejected. The few birds that had returned to their spring, summer trees were too small and too afraid of crows to be any fun. And the gulls on the coast wanted nothing to do with Kingston. Worst of all, it seemed that Kingston never wanted to hang out with other crows. My poor bird was a social outcast. I decided a fresh batch of hardboiled eggs would cheer him up. I used my afternoon break to walk down to the Corner Market, a bursting at the seams, immaculately organized little 'everything' store at the corner of Harbor Lane and Pickford Way, right next to the Port Danby Police Station and across from Franki's Diner.

I walked past the tinted windows of the police station and glanced inside. Detective Briggs' car was out front, signaling that he was inside his office doing paperwork. I knew for a fact that he preferred to be out on duty than stuck behind his desk. The half open blinds gave me a striped view of the front desk. Hilda, the wonderful woman who kept the station running smoothly, had taped a string of paper hearts across the bleak gray front of the counter. No matter what the holiday, Hilda made an attempt to bring cheer into the grimly decorated police station. I passed the station and came upon a much cheerier building, the always bustling Corner Market. The outside of the store was coated with white and blue lacquer paint and bright blue awnings stretched out over the rolling carts that were usually piled with the day's produce specials. Today Gigi and Tom Upton, the store owners had filled the carts with the last of the winter's citrus fruit, tangerines and succulent looking mandarin oranges.

I stopped to pick a few oranges and breathe in the savory, sweet and tangy smells drifting out of the store. I was concentrating on finding the best smelling oranges and didn't look up when the door to the store opened and a customer walked out.

"Lacey?"

I glanced up from the produce. It seemed I was having one long day of awkward moments, starting with my lovely robe fashion show. Then there was the stilted, slow to smooth out conversation with Detective Briggs outside the bakery. And now I was standing face to face with the man I'd almost married and who my last words to had been, 'I never want to see you again'. And yet, there we were standing not more than twenty inches apart, and both at a loss for words.

Jacob was one of those men whose appearance was so fluid, it was hard to describe him with exact terms. Certain attributes were solid and required no objective opinion. He was tall, a few inches past six foot, and his shoulders were impressively broad. But his hair could change from tawny to brown to dark brown depending on the length of it. It seemed he'd opted for a close cut along the sides with some short, almost teenager looking spikes on top. He was a thirty something trying to hold on to his twenties. Even his eyes changed color according to the light. They were anywhere from gray to green. I'd discovered a few months after our engage-

35

ment that his eyes grew particularly green whenever he was lying. Near the end of our relationship they were like two brilliant emeralds, a stone I'd never wanted to wear since. His nose was noticeably red, which meant he was suffering from a cold. And suffering was a light word for the way Jacob acted when he was sick.

"Jacob." I dropped the oranges back onto the cart. "I heard you were in town."

"Yes." His succinct answer left another clumsy moment of silence.

I looked down at the box of tea and bear shaped squeeze bottle of clover honey in his hand. "Grandma Georgio's cure for a sore throat?" I'd brewed more than my share of tea honey concoctions for him when he was under the weather.

A cloud of menthol laden breath puffed out of his mouth as he pushed the last slivers of a throat lozenge around his tongue. He moved his scarf up higher around his neck. "I should have taken my doctor's advice and gotten rid of those blasted tonsils."

At least I'd gotten the conversation moving and out of the uncomfortable hole of silence. Even if we were talking about his blasted tonsils.

"I get colds way too often. I woke up yesterday with a raw throat and this damp coastal air isn't helping matters." Had he always been such a 'delicate flower'? Maybe my initial crush on the man had blinded me to all of his many flaws.

"It is rather unusual for you to travel along on a photo shoot. What made you go this time?" I vaguely tried to reflect on whether or not I was fishing for a particular answer. But the truth was, I couldn't remember even one time when he had dragged along with the photography crew for a photo shoot. He usually always sent an assistant, like Hazel, along to make sure things ran smoothly.

"To be honest, I needed a break from the everyday drudgery of running a business."

"Ah, yes. I heard you were in charge now. I can see where that would make life harder and a little more tedious. Although, I'm running a business myself, and I absolutely love it."

His mouth drooped some, and he seemed to be disappointed by my declaration. "So, you're happy then?"

"Very."

He nodded faintly. "I'm glad for you, Lacey. You deserve to be happy." For the first time since our breakup I detected a genuine moment of regret in his tone. He had been angered and defensive when I'd confronted him about being unfaithful, but I'd never seen regret. It was both satisfying and a little sad to see now. Especially with him looking miserable from a cold.

"Thank you, Jacob. I wish you all the best too. Really." Somehow we managed to initiate a stiff, brief hug. He held the tea in one hand and the honey in the other, but he seemed determined to pull it off. As his arms wrapped around me, it occurred to me that there was nothing. I could have been hugging any casual acquaintance and not the man I was once set to marry. There wasn't even the slightest twinge of emotion or nostalgia or heartache. The only thing familiar was the faint scent of his cologne, a scent he'd had custom made by the company's chemists. It was particularly familiar to me because I'd helped formulate the subtle woodsy fragrance. It was a blend of cedar wood and cypress tinged with the citrus twist of bergamot oil. Jacob and I had been at that early, nervous stomach flutter stage in our relationship. He was thrilled that his girlfriend would actually create his cologne, guaranteeing that I would love it. As much as I enjoyed the smell of the cologne, I never had the heart to confess that for someone like me, any scent could be overwhelming.

A car swept past, making a sharp U-turn at the corner and spraying some fine grit onto the sidewalk. I released my hold on Jacob and glanced out to the street. Detective Briggs' car rolled past.

I lifted my hand to wave, but he had turned his face back toward the road. His car hurtled north on Harbor Lane.

Jacob straightened and clutched his tea and honey against him. "I better get back up to the location. It's a unique setting. I think it'll work. We decided to go with a sort of gothic feel to the whole thing. It's our newest fragrance, Ode to Love. I'd love to get your opinion on it. Wendy, our new perfumer, has a pretty good nose." He smiled weakly. "It's not the Lacey Pinkerton million dollar nose, but I think she's got a handle on things. You should come up and see everyone. Hazel has already told everyone that she saw you so you're sort of on the hook now."

"I'll visit later today, after I close up shop. My house is walking distance from the Hawksworth Manor."

He nodded. "I'll bet that was a selling point for you. You always did like ghost stories and haunted houses. And if that big, old mausoleum isn't haunted, then the ghosts around here are missing out big time." His mood had brightened since he walked out of the market looking miserable with a cold. "It was really nice talking to you again, Lacey. I wish we hadn't parted in such a bad way."

"It was nice talking to you too, Jacob. And I'm sorry too. I'll see all of you later, up at the manor."

CHAPTER 7

*L*ight was fading fast as I drove up Myrtle Place to home. Kingston paced the top of the passenger seat, anxious to get to his comfy perch for the night. Along with the pointed turret tops of the manor up on Maple Hill, I could see the glow of Lydia's photography lights. They were still working. It wasn't too surprising. Lydia was a perfectionist. She liked to take pictures at various times of the day to find the right natural light for the photos.

I decided to take Kingston home and walk up the hill for a quick visit.

The sun was just disappearing behind the roofs of the town as I reached the top of Maple Hill. The research I'd been doing on the Hawksworth murders had been mostly at the library and in the evidence room of the police station. I hadn't been to the actual site for several months, ever since my disappointing self-guided tour through the museum of artifacts the town had set up in the old gardener's shed on the estate. The steeply pitched gable roofs had even less shingles than a few months ago. And there was so much dust on the leaded window panes, it was hard to discern them from the dust covered facade. Some of the thick, bulbous balustrades that lined the long second story balcony had been broken, making it look like a row of bad teeth. The one improvement was the noticeable lack of chain link fence around the front of the house. It looked far less dreary without the safety barrier.

The manor had been built over a century ago high above the town on a large parcel of land, large enough to accommodate the six trucks and trailers that had been set up for the week long stay. Generators provided electricity. The company never spared any expense when it came to their marketing team. Magazine layouts were the perfume industry's number one form of advertising, and a successful photo shoot was a top priority.

Lydia's crew had set up large screens and lights. Lydia, herself, was still hunched in front of the tripod as I walked up. Jacob was nowhere in sight. Hazel was sitting on the steps of one of the trailers eating a burger. She waved for me to join her.

I walked a wide berth around the photo action, not wanting to break concentration. Jasper and Autumn, the stunningly gorgeous couple who had been the faces of Georgio's Perfume for the last three years, were in a romantic embrace as Lydia called out cues for different poses.

I sat on the step next to Hazel, and she offered me an onion ring. "I'm so glad you came. They're almost finished, so don't leave until you get a chance to say hello."

The onion ring was cold, but it reminded me that I was hungry for dinner. "I don't see Jacob. Is he feeling worse?"

Hazel leaned aside to look at me on the narrow step. "How did you know he was sick?"

"I guess he didn't mention that he ran into me down at the market. He was buying the ingredients for Grandma Georgio's sore throat elixir."

Hazel elbowed me with a laugh. "It cracks me up when he calls it that, like it's some special, groundbreaking brew. I don't think there's a grandma from here to Siberia that hasn't prescribed tea and honey for a sore throat."

I laughed. "I've heard that the recipe is the first page in the grandmother's handbook." We laughed again, and I helped myself to another cold onion ring.

"And in answer to your question," Hazel continued. "Jacob was feeling worse. He fell asleep in his trailer hours ago. We have rooms reserved at the nearby hotel, but something tells me we'll all just camp out here for the night." She rolled her eyes. "Lydia wants to get a few sunrise shots. The view from this hill really is like a postcard."

I gazed out at the coastline several miles away. From Maple Hill I could see all the way down to the tallest masts on boats in the Pickford Marina. Off to the right, with a good deal of searching, I could see the white sands of Pickford Beach. The horizon line was blurred by a wall of incoming coastal fog.

"Lydia might be disappointed in the sunrise. That horizon looks a little ominous tonight. That usually means the entire town will wake to a heavy blanket of fog."

"You know Lydia. She'll consider it a sign that the tone needs to be more gothic. She'll just run with it."

"That's true."

Lydia Harris was a no-nonsense photographer who could be as brilliant and hard to please as any talented artist. Sometimes she had a fit if mother nature was messing around too much, making the sunlight as fickle as a fair weather friend. Other times, she invited the challenge. She was a taller than average woman, at least five ten with her own sense of style. Today she wore a flowing, gauzy tunic paired with leather boots. Her long hair was piled up on her head with metallic clips shoved in at various locations to keep it all secured.

Hazel and I watched her finish the shoot. "That's a wrap,

people. Be ready for a sunrise start tomorrow." The mention of an early start sent a grumble around the crew.

Hazel sighed. "That means one of us will be saddled with the task of waking Jasper out of his sleeping pill coma."

"Does he still suffer from that terrible insomnia?"

"I think it's worse than ever. He takes pills to nap during the day and then he drinks those high-octane caffeine drinks to stay awake."

Lydia let her assistants clean up. She headed over to Hazel and me with a broad smile.

"Pink, I heard you were coming to visit." Lydia was one of the people, who not only preferred to call me by my nickname, I was fairly certain she didn't even remember my real name.

I hopped up and gave her a hug.

Hazel handed Lydia her burger. "I got it with pickles and grilled onions, just the way you like it." Haze, as everyone around the office at Georgio's Perfume called her, was a people pleaser through and through. And even though she was a bit of a gossip (and there was plenty to gossip about at Georgio's) she rarely said a cross word about anyone. Unless they firmly deserved it, like Olivia from accounting who was constantly cooking fish in the lounge microwave at lunch, even after Hazel had made a beautiful sign in a polite tone, a tone Hazel had perfected for office memos. The sign read "If at all possible, please avoid cooking foods with strong odors like fish." It couldn't have been more subtle and passive, yet it seemed Olivia took offense and made sure to eat fish every day for a week. Until she finally realized that everyone was avoiding eating lunch with her. Even her closest confidante, Rachel, from marketing had taken to eating at her desk.

Lydia unwrapped her burger. "Thanks, Haze. I'm starved. We should have ordered one for Pink."

"Oh no, I can't stay long."

"Come see who's here." Lydia's tunic flowed like wings as she

42

waved over Jasper and Autumn, both dressed in elegant black formal wear. Autumn looked spectacular in a close fitting black sequin gown. She'd pulled on a warm coat. Autumn was in her early twenties with skin like pure cream and eyes that took up half her face, the other half being taken by full lips. She had more personality and charm than her male counterpart, Jasper, but she also tended to get whiny when a shoot was taking too long. Her hair had been dyed blonde for the pictures, which washed her out some, but it seemed the makeup artist had sprayed on a sun-kissed tan color to make her look as if she'd just stepped off a summer beach.

"Lacey, right?" Autumn asked, even though I was sure she knew my name.

"Right."

Jasper huffed and shook his head. "How on earth could you possibly forget her name? Lacey is a perfume industry legend." Jasper bounded forward for a hug.

Jasper Edmonton was the male half of the face of Georgio's Perfume. He was one of those men who spent far more time in front of the mirror than would be considered healthy or normal. There was no denying that he was a sight to see, especially all polished up for a photo shoot. His dark brows looked as if they'd been painted on over wedgewood blue eyes that were framed by thick black lashes. His nose and chin were so perfectly symmetrical and in balance with the rest of him, I'd heard Lydia, the photographer complain that she had to tweak his photos sometimes because Jasper looked as if he'd stepped out of a Ken doll mold. He was too perfect to look real.

Lydia, with her artist's eye had been trying to get the company to switch models for years, complaining Jasper and Autumn were so attractive they were dull. I had to admit she was right. And, as was often the case with people who were gifted with nature's perfection, they tended to be a touch self-centered and pompous.

And Jasper followed the stereotype as perfectly as he smiled for the camera.

"So, Lacey, are you actually happy in this tiny, dull town?" Jasper eyed my head of curls with an amused grin. "Looks like you gave up the curl fight against this coastal climate."

"I think she looks adorable," Hazel piped up.

I nodded at her. "Thank you, Hazel. Adorable wasn't exactly the look I was hoping for, but I'll take it." I turned back to Jasper. "Yes, once I understood the fulfillment of being my own boss and running my own company, I found spending time in front of a mirror was a waste."

Jasper's mouth straightened, and he bristled at my comment.

"Burn," Autumn said with a laugh. "Well, I'm going into my trailer to take off this stupid dress." She cast me a perfunctory smile and floated away in waves of black sequins.

"I've got to head home too," I said. "My pets are waiting for dinner."

"Do you still have the crow?" Lydia asked between burger bites.

"I sure do. And he's as ornery as ever."

Jasper glanced around. "How did you get here? I don't see a car."

"I walked. I live just down the hill."

"In one of those tiny houses?" Jasper asked, not even bothering to hide his distaste. If possible, it seemed he'd grown even more pompous.

"Yes, Jasper, in one of those tiny houses. And I've never been happier. Good night, everyone."

I headed down the hill to my tiny, cozy, wonderful house and thought, I sure didn't miss the perfume industry.

CHAPTER 8

I'd had a pet crow long enough that I should have been able to anticipate his every move. And yet, after breakfast, I'd blithely opened the front door so Kingston could cruise the neighborhood and stretch his wings. But instead of his usual route along Loveland Terrace, which always ended in the crow sweeping in and scaring all the smaller birds away from Helen Voight's bird feeder, an escapade that usually earned him a hearty lecture from Helen, Kingston swept over the front yard and turned sharply to head up towards Maple Hill. My clever bird had already puzzled out that the activity on the hill would surely result in delicious morsels of food dropped carelessly on freshly thawed ground.

I'd said my hellos the night before, and a second visit was not on my list of things to do, especially not so early and so soon after seeing everyone. But I knew Kingston, who was far too at ease with humans, was quite capable of causing havoc. Or, at the very least, some frayed nerves.

I pulled on my coat and boots and trudged back up Maple Hill to Hawksworth Manor. I was pleasantly surprised to find that Kingston had maintained some level of decorum. He was scuffling around behind the trailers, out of sight of the donut munching humans, waiting politely for his chance to swoop in and clean up the crumbs.

Lydia was in the middle of a photo session. She had moved the lights and screens closer to the manor. Autumn and Jasper were posing on the rickety front steps leading up to the front door.

Jacob stood nearby watching the shoot. He hadn't seen me walk up. In fact, it seemed only Kingston had noticed me. I was considering the possibility that I could get my bird down off the site before anyone saw me when I heard my name.

"Well, if it isn't Lacey and her priceless nose." Alexander approached me with a chocolate donut. "These were your favorite as I recall."

I'd already eaten but didn't want to be rude, considering he'd remembered what my favorite donut flavor was when Autumn couldn't even remember my name.

"Thank you. I'll save it for my coffee break."

Alexander waved his arm around with a flourish. "Great location, and I owe it all to you and your magical Instagram account."

For as long as I worked at Georgio's, Alexander Nettles had been the location scout for the advertising team. He had a terrific eye for drama. He was always somewhat dramatic himself and tended to use wild hand gestures to get his point across. He was always checking out the scenery through a half rectangle he created with his two hands. He was constantly changing his style, and it seemed he'd landed somewhere between hipster and bohemian with flannel, suspenders, rolled jeans and a flat brimmed hat. His beard was longer than usual too.

"Well, my Instagram account is flattered, Alexander. I'm thrilled that my pictures inspired you. I think Port Danby is wonderful. Of course, I'm rather biased."

"Lacey, I didn't expect to see you up here this morning." The scent of menthol wafted over my shoulder.

I turned and smiled up at Jacob. He looked less miserable than the day before, but his nose was a Rudolph red. "I wasn't expecting it either." I looked in the direction where I'd last seen Kingston and saw him slowly making his way toward the catering table. "I had to follow a certain scamp who has his bird heart set on donut crumbs."

"Kingston," Jacob said with far more admiration than I'd ever heard from him when reciting my bird's name.

His name, coming from a somewhat familiar voice, caused the crow to shift his focus away from the donuts and toward the group of people talking about him. Of course, I was still holding a donut, chocolate. His favorite.

"I can't believe you still have that crow, but then you did love that bird. I was always jealous of him for that." Jacob pulled a shiny silver cigarette case from his coat pocket.

"And I can't believe you still smoke those clove cigarettes. They used to make my eyes water."

Alexander cleared his throat. "This sounds like my cue to leave."

"Thank you for the donut."

He hurried off.

I turned back to Jacob.

Jacob put the cigarette back into the box.

"Don't put it away on my account. I just came to round up my bird. I need to get ready for work."

He placed the box back into his coat pocket. "My throat is still sore. I don't think the clove cigarettes will help. And everything tastes weird after sucking on a lozenge."

"Lacey," Hazel called excitedly as she flew down the portable steps of the catering trailer. She hurried across the lot waving her arms, causing Kingston to take off and head for a safe perch above.

Hazel pointed up to the tree. "Was that Kingston?"

"Yep, I followed him up here to make sure he wasn't terrorizing the crew." I smiled and turned to catch Jacob's reaction to my comment, but he was no longer standing next to me. I spotted his tall head back at the viewing spot he'd staked out for watching the photo shoot.

Hazel took my arm. She noticed the abrupt departure as well. "He's been in a bad mood because Autumn and Jasper have been unusually handsy and flirty with each other during the photo sessions." She was practically mumbling, even though Jacob was out of ear shot.

We moved a little closer to watch Lydia and her models at work.

"I can't stay long. Was Lydia upset about the fog cover this morning?"

"Nope. My prediction was right," Hazel said proudly. "Lydia thought the gloomy fog added to the gothic ambience of the place. But it took them forever to get enough lighting up."

Autumn was dressed in a long dark pink off the shoulder gown and Jasper in a black suit and tie. From our vantage point it seemed they'd put extra zeal into the passionate embrace Lydia had asked for. Autumn giggled and leaned her head back, nearly dislodging the rhinestone trimmed bun at the back of her head. Jasper placed a kiss on her neck, and Autumn giggled some more.

"Take this seriously, Autumn. This whole damn thing is costing a fortune," Jacob barked. He finished his angry command by pressing his hand to his throat.

"Oh boy, Autumn is really pushing all his buttons today." Hazel's expression bordered on a satisfied smirk but then she washed it away quickly, aware that I'd noticed it.

"He's obviously not feeling well. (I added, for some reason, on

Jacob's behalf.) He gets grumpy when he's sick. I didn't realize Jacob and Autumn were that serious. She doesn't seem like his type. Or vice versa."

"It's been an on again, off again thing for awhile." An irritated huff followed. "Autumn is a great manipulator of men. Almost have to sort of admire her for it."

"As I recall, Jasper and Autumn were an item when they first signed with Georgio's Perfume." I looked back to check on Kingston. He was still perched in a tree.

Hazel leaned closer, even though no one else could hear our conversation. "Yes, but it turned out that Jasper was just using Autumn. They had met at Fashion Week in Paris. Jasper badly wanted to sign with the big New York modeling agency that Autumn had been with since her teens. The breakup was sudden and not amicable. Or at least that was what I heard. They used to fight all the time. It is amazing they have any on-screen chemistry at all."

"They sure seem to have it now," I noted. I glanced in Jacob's direction. He had lit up the clove cigarette anyway, and he was puffing angrily away on it.

"That's a wrap for this morning," Lydia called. "You two need to rest and then get back into makeup. You both look like something that floated in with that horrible fog this morning."

Jasper offered Autumn a gentlemanly hand down the steps of the porch. She accepted with a broad smile.

"Seems like Autumn's forgiven him for the unseemly breakup," I said quietly as Jasper headed our direction.

Jasper's face grew tight as he struggled to loosen the necktie. He stopped in front of Hazel. "Get this stupid thing off of me. It's choking the life out of me." He'd asked so rudely, I wanted to step in and offer him a few choice words, but it wasn't my place. I no longer worked for Georgio's Perfume.

Hazel responded immediately and loosened the neck tie. Jasper stomped off without a thank you. She offered me a weak smile. "He's always grumpy because he's always tired."

"That's very conciliatory of you, Hazel. I was going to say that some people get wiser and better with age, and some just get more obnoxious."

Hazel laughed. "Boy, do I miss having you around the office, Lacey. Just not the same without you."

CHAPTER 9

I finished up with some dull paperwork and was lured to the front of the shop by a strong fragrance. "I smell sage."

"Good call." Ryder scooped up several handfuls of dried sage leaves from the mound he had dumped on the island. "My mom's sage plants needed trimming. I've been drying it in the garage. That takes some of the bite out of the smell."

"Yes, bite is a good word for it. I confess, I love the taste of sage in Thanksgiving stuffing, but the smell can be overwhelming for sensitive noses."

Ryder pulled the spool of rustic twine off its spindle on the wall. "If you don't mind, I'm going to make bundles of the dried leaves. Many ancient cultures burn dried sage to help cleanse their spirits and aura. I thought it would be a fun novelty item for the store. I'll make a cool sign to go with it."

"Absolutely. I'm all for cleaning spirits and auras."

"That's what I love about you, boss. You never poo poo my ideas. No matter how bizarre they might be."

I laughed. "Just call me the non-poo poo boss."

Ryder's eyes rounded.

I pointed to my ear. "Yes, that sounded bad out loud. And just for the record—my digestive tract is fine."

I walked over to the stack of Valentine's orders piled up next to the cash register. "Wow, customers really like your bouquets, Ryder."

"Seems that way. That reminds me, we need to order more yellow mugs for the *chillin'* bouquet. Apparently more people than ever are slow to make commitments these days."

"That does seem to be the case. I'll go pull up the purchase order and buy a dozen more." I headed back to the office.

"Hey, Lacey, there's that lady again. She popped her head into the shop earlier while you were in the office. She didn't want to disturb you, but I think she's back."

I stepped back out of the short hallway just as Hazel entered the store. She was holding two of Lester's coffee mocha specials. "I don't want to keep you from your work, Lacey, but I hoped you could take a quick coffee break with me. The nice white haired man next door has the coolest tables and chairs. I've never seen counter high tables out on a sidewalk. And he has these marvelous heating lamps, so the whole place glows with warmth."

"Yes, Lester puts a great deal of thought into his sidewalk tables." I winked at Ryder. It hadn't taken long for Ryder to figure out that a full blown table war was going on around our humble little shop. "Ryder, I'll just be ten minutes."

"Sure thing."

Hazel stretched up to see what he was working on. "Hmm, is that dried sage? I hear it's good for the soul to meditate while burning sage."

Ryder nodded. "Yes, it is."

Hazel handed me a coffee. "Thank you so much. I love Lester's coffee mocha." We walked out to the sidewalk. I took a quick look over my shoulder to make sure Elsie didn't see me walking over to Lester's table area. I'd found it was always best if I played neutral, the proverbial Switzerland, when it came to the table war. I tried to encourage good ideas and discourage bad ones, like the cardboard Mr. Darcy. I also avoided sitting on either side.

We sat on the table closest to the Coffee Hutch. Lester instantly caught sight of me and waved enthusiastically from behind his counter. With any luck, he wouldn't mention the visit to Elsie. (Who was I kidding?)

Hazel and I hoisted ourselves up onto the tall stools. I cradled the hot cup of coffee in my hands to warm them.

Hazel took a sip. "Hmm, that hits the spot. So . . . I got the rest of the scoop on the Jasper and Autumn relationship from Lydia. It became quite apparent that Jasper was just using Autumn to get into the agency and once he signed, he broke it off." She shook her head. "As you saw today, there is always so much drama at Georgio's Perfume. Even so, I'm sure I'll miss it when I leave."

Her last comment caused me to suck in my coffee. I covered a cough and swallowed. "What do you mean? Are you leaving Georgio's Perfume?"

She looked up at me in surprise. "Didn't I tell you? I was sure I mentioned it. I got an executive assistant job at Tremaine's Fashion House."

I was dumbfounded. Hazel had been at Georgio's Perfume for years, and she was considered irreplaceable. "Hazel, I'm both shocked and excited. This has to be very hard on Jacob. He relies on you for everything."

Her cheeks ballooned with her grin. "That's so kind of you, Lacey. But Jacob understood that it was time for me to move on." She reached over and took my hand. "But maybe don't mention it to him. He's in such a terrible mood with his cold and with the way Autumn has been teasing him, trying to make him jealous."

"So is that what's happening? The flirty smiles and giggles we saw earlier at the photo shoot. She's trying to make him jealous?"

"Sure looks that way to me." She sucked in a breath. "I wonder if it has to do with you. Maybe she wants to keep his attention off of you."

I shook my head. "Hazel, that is a very flattering assessment, but it's also very wrong. I assure you Autumn is not the slightest bit threatened by my presence. She's young. She is still just playing games with him. He's a grown man. He'll figure it out. Once he gets his head clear of that cold."

Hazel hunched forward and lowered her voice, signaling a juicy nugget was about to follow. Completely unnecessary considering we were alone at the tables. "If you ask me, I think Jacob is done with Jasper. I think he's considering just paying off the rest of Jasper's contract so he can get a new male face for the perfume." She unrolled her shoulders. "But that's just pure speculation on my part."

"Well, if anyone can speculate about Jacob's next move, it's you, Hazel. You know him better than anyone."

"I have to agree." She lifted her cup. "It's so great to be able to talk to you again, Lacey."

"It is indeed." I lifted my cup and we toasted with our coffees.

CHAPTER 10

*E*arly in the morning, I'd promised myself to carve out a section of time in the afternoon for a trip to the library, a quaint but impressive library in the neighboring town of Chesterton. The bookshelves were brimming with fiction and non-fiction, but I was there to visit the back room that was filled with decades of newspaper articles and, in particular, preserved copies of the century old Chesterton Gazette.

I pulled into the lot and nearly blushed with shame at how long it had been since I'd been there. The two evergreen saplings that were mere spindles on my last visit had thickened in trunk and pine needles. I'd been remiss in my self-appointed duty of murder mystery detective. Almost since I'd first heard of the terrible murder-suicide that wiped out the entire Hawksworth family, I had wanted to learn more about it. And the more I discovered, the more it seemed that the events of that terrible night had gone very differently than stated in the final police report, a report that was comically brief and simple for such a horrendous crime.

I headed up the stone path to the barn red building and walked through the blue front door. Tilly Stratton, the head librarian, was easy to recognize with her overlong front teeth and her bowl haircut. The odd haircut was either extremely unfashionable or so unique it could be considered fashionable, like those strange, outlandish accessories that designers paraded down the runways in New York and Paris. But given the rest of Tilly Statton's attire, a prim gray sweater, blouse and gray skirt, it was easy to lean away from the high fashion theory. I silently chastised myself for even thinking unkindly about her appearance as she flashed me a gracious smile.

"Hello." She squinted behind her round glasses. "The Chesterton Gazette and the Hawksworth Murders, right?"

"Wow, that's impressive considering it's been a few months since I've been here. And I'm embarrassed to say that out loud. As a kid, I spent a lot of summer hours at the local library. I miss those carefree days."

Tilly reached into a drawer and pulled out a set of keys. "I'll bet you read a lot of mysteries."

"Once again. Impressive." I followed her through the stacks where tables and chairs rounded off every row of books. Tilly stopped to pick up a book that had fallen off a shelf. She tucked it back into its place, and we continued through to the back room where the local archives were stored.

The musty scent of old paper and ink struck us as Tilly opened the door to the back room. The smell was slightly overwhelming, which meant the door had probably not been opened recently. Several tables and chairs sat in the center of the room. The shelves that lined the three walls were stacked high with newspapers. Each shelf was labeled with a date and the name of the periodical stored there.

Tilly walked to the table and pulled a pair of latex gloves from the box, a precaution to keep oil off the crispy, old newspapers. She handed me the gloves. "Remember to wear these and use as many note cards as you like. Please leave the newspapers on the table so I can shelve them when you're finished. By the way—" she walked to a set of file drawers near the door. "These drawers contain microfiches."

My mouth opened in surprise.

My reaction caused her to laugh. "Yes, I know. We are probably the last library in the United States to still have some documents on microfiche." As she spoke, she walked to the nearby closet and opened the door. "And a microfiche machine. It's kind of a dinosaur, but it still works. The documents stored in the cabinet are mostly birth, death and marriage certificates from the early part of the last century. We just haven't had time to transfer anything to digital storage. But you're welcome to look through them. They are nicely organized alphabetically."

"Great. I think that's all I need then. Thank you so much."

Tilly walked out. I pulled my previous note cards out of my coat pocket to remind myself of all the pertinent information I'd found so far. My short tour through the gardener's shed, where the town had set a few personal items from the home to lure tourists to the site, had produced one valuable item, a police photograph. The photograph of the freshly murdered Bertram and Jill Hawksworth showed Mr. Hawksworth, the purported murderer, with a gun in his right hand. But a 1901 newspaper clipping I'd found in the archives showed a very much alive Bertram Hawksworth signing the documents for his future shipyard, a shipyard that never got built. He was holding the nib pen in his left hand, which meant he was left-handed. It was a clear indication that the gun had been placed in his right hand, something the first officer investigating the case had noted. But that officer was transferred to another station right after the murder so he was never able to follow up on the inconsistency. The next person in charge signed off on the case, closing it as murder and suicide.

As I pulled on the thin latex gloves, I walked along the shelves reading the dates. The murder took place in October of 1906. I decided to concentrate on the years between 1901 and 1906. Mr. Hawksworth's shipyard was never built. A quick tour of the coastline along Port Danby was proof of that, but there had to be more to it. The construction of a big shipyard would have meant considerable change for a small town like Port Danby. It would have meant jobs and expansion of towns and neighborhoods, just as much as it would have meant chaos and a disruption of the otherwise picturesque and serene coastline.

A second 1901 newspaper picture had shown a jovial, excited Bertram Hawksworth about to break ground for the shipyard. I decided to thumb through the headlines for the year 1902. Detective Briggs had mentioned that he'd heard a court order had stopped the building of the shipyard. I hoped to find something about it. A large financial endeavor like a shipyard had to come with some political or business enemies. Having his big plans cut short must have been devastating to Bertram Hawksworth.

I'd worn my strongest reading glasses. My eyes passed back and forth over the headlines, skimming names and places hoping to come across some important keywords. After some perseverance and an itchy nose from decades of old dust, I spotted an important headline; *Hawksworth Shipyard Dead in the Water.* I pulled the newspaper free of the stack and took it to the table.

The front page picture was of a stout older man with a ramrod straight, imperious posture, not uncommon for a Victorian photo. He was sitting behind a large desk. A woman was standing next to him holding a ledger of some kind under her arm. The man's big, pillowy face was lined with fuzzy sideburns. His expression was noticeably smug. The paper had yellowed a great deal and print quality was lacking at the turn of the century. I lowered my face to read the caption. "Mayor Harvard Price and Port Danby treasurer Jane Price."

It seemed I was looking at Mayor Price's relative. I knew that the Price family had held the mayor's seat for many years. Now I was seeing proof of it. The more I looked at the picture, the more I could see a smidgen of Harlan Price in the man's face.

I read the article, which was a short summary of the court's decision to block the building of the Hawksworth Shipyard. Mayor Harvard Price had asked the courts to intervene, deciding it was in the best interest of the community to stop the shipyard. The journalist noted that it had been a very risky move on the part of the mayor, as many folks from the surrounding towns were looking forward to working at the shipyard. There was no mention of a comment from Bertram Hawksworth, but I could only imagine how angry and disappointed he was after losing in court. Maybe he snapped after that. Maybe the loss drove him to insanity, which eventually drove him to kill his whole family.

I sat back. What were the mayor's motives for stopping something that surely would have made the town prosper? Yes, a massive project like a shipyard would have brought a great deal of pandemonium to the town, but surely, there were enough benefits to look past the risks.

I focused back on the picture and on the woman. The severe early century hairstyles, drab clothing and picture quality always made it hard to judge the age of people in old photos, especially when the image was printed in a newspaper. But it seemed the woman, Jane Price, was quite young. And while the name could have been a coincidence, I could only assume that she was related to Harvard Price.

I stood up and walked back to the shelf, deciding to thumb through for other interesting headlines. I needed to head back to the shop, but I allowed myself a few more minutes of sleuthing. I thumbed through the rest of 1902 and was almost pulled in twice to read about other interesting events in town, but I needed to stay focused. I'd come back one day when there was more time to browse through the articles.

I was halfway through the 1903 stack and just about to call it a day, when my eyes traveled past the words Port Danby treasurer. I pulled the paper free and carried it to the table. A small man in a vest sporting a long, curly moustache was grinning stiffly at the camera. He was holding a ledger under his arm. I read the short caption below the picture. "Fielding Smith has been appointed to the position of Port Danby treasurer. The position had gone unfilled for several months since Miss Jane Price, daughter of Harvard Price, moved unexpectedly out of town."

I wrote a few things down on my note card and pushed it back into my pocket. All in all, not a hugely successful day in the archives, but I now had a bit more information about the quick demise of the Hawksworth Shipyard. And since the source of the demise was none other than Mayor Harvard Price, it was easy to conclude that the Hawksworths and the Prices were not good friends after that. Was it possible money, power and revenge were the motives behind the murders, rather than passion, infidelity and jealousy?

CHAPTER 11

*R*yder had gone home and I was shutting off lights to close up for the night when Hazel's face popped up in the window. Hazel and I had spent time together when I worked at Georgio's but most of that time was during office hours, like at lunch or on coffee break. But it seemed she was in need of a friend more than ever. Perhaps she was beginning to feel a little anxious about starting a new job. She'd been at Georgio's for her entire career.

I opened the door and she walked in before I could mention that I was locking up. Kingston chirped an irritated, throaty sound. His dinnertime had just been delayed.

The weather was dark and chilly due to a storm just off shore waiting to douse the town with cold rain, but Hazel was only wearing a sweater over her blouse and jeans. The sweater was a bright blue paisley knit, one that I was certain I'd seen in the window of the Mod Frock, a vintage clothing boutique in town.

Hazel seemed extra energetic as if she'd had a great deal of coffee. She held out her arms. "Don't you love it? I picked it up at this wonderful little shop at the end of Harbor Lane. It's called Mod Frock. Don't you just love that name?" she was practically singing her words. "Have you been there? Everything looks like it came from the sixties. I love that era. There hasn't been a decade like the sixties since . . . since ever!" She finished with a spirited laugh.

Perhaps it wasn't anxiety about the new job but pure delight.

Hazel finally noticed that most of the lights were out. "Oh, I'm sorry, I stopped you on your way out. I was just so thrilled with my new sweater, and since everyone else went out to dinner, I decided I'd come show you my purchase. I just love this town. No wonder you are so happy here. Is this crazy? I was thinking about coming back here next week just to have tea with Mr. Darcy. I do love Colin Firth."

Grr, that Elsie. What had she done?

"Oh, Hazel, I hate to break that bubble, but Colin Firth will not be here. It's just a cardboard cutout of the actor created from a still of him when he played Mr. Darcy."

Hazel's brows knitted together, and her spirits were noticeably dampened. "I feel so foolish. I seem to be doing silly things a lot lately. I must have misread the flyer."

"No, no you didn't. And I've already lectured my neighbor about false advertising. I assure you, you aren't the first person to think he'd actually be here. And unfortunately for my friend, Elsie, I'm certain you won't be the last. But you are right. I was just on my way out. I need to get this crow home for his dinner or he'll start giving me the evil eye."

Hazel took a few discrete steps away from Kingston's perch in the window. "Too late, I think he's already doing it." She stopped. "How can you tell? He always looks kind of evil with those shiny black eyes."

"Trust me, when you've been around him long enough, you can tell the difference. I'm just going to grab my purse."

I walked back into the office to get my purse and keys.

"How much is the sage?" Hazel called to the back. "I'm in need of a good aura cleansing."

Hazel was picking up each of the twine wrapped bundles and smelling them. She crinkled her nose at one and held it up. "How much?"

"It's on the house."

"Are you sure?"

"Of course. They are just trimmings from a sage plant." We walked out. Hazel screamed as Kingston swooped past us and landed on the top of my car. She was definitely wound a little tighter than usual.

"Sorry, I forgot to warn you to duck. Do you need a ride to Maple Hill or the hotel?"

"Nope, I borrowed the van. It's parked down by that wonderful boutique. I might just have to stop myself from going in there again. Otherwise, I'll blow my bank account on vintage clothes."

"I can give you a ride to the van."

"No, that's fine. The fresh air and walk will do me good."

A breeze whistled along Harbor Lane. I zipped up my coat. "It looks like rain tomorrow."

"That's what the weatherman said." Hazel rolled her eyes. "That means a delay in the work, and everyone will be grumpy while they sit around waiting for the rain to stop. And Jacob is already grumpy because of his cold."

"He's not feeling any better?"

She shook her head as she buttoned the sweater. "I guess I better get back to the van. It's colder than I thought out here. See you tomorrow, Lacey. Maybe we can do lunch or something before we leave."

"Absolutely."

CHAPTER 12

The local news weatherman had issued warnings of a downpour along the coastal towns, but other than a few minutes of heavy drops on the roof, it was mostly a fizzling drizzle. Even my windshield wipers were scoffing at the forecast as they chugged across mostly dry glass on my way down Myrtle Place. Still, I was without my feathered partner for the day. Kingston had taken one look out the front door and gone back to his warm, dry cage.

The sky remained dark with the threat of more precipitation, and it seemed we'd only see intermittent sun all day. But Ryder was wearing a sunshiney smile as we met at the front door of the shop. He was covered head to toe in rain gear, with a hooded yellow slicker pulled up over his head. His long wet bangs were plastered against his forehead.

"You look as if you went out on an early morning fishing expedition," I noted as we walked inside.

He gave his boots an extra rub on the outside mat before entering. "Not a fishing expedition, but I did catch some awesome rainbow pictures." He pulled his phone out of his pocket, and we both started the ritual of un-layering from our winter gear. "I went down to Pickford Beach this morning to take pictures and test out the waterproof claim on my new phone. You'd be surprised how many people are out there on the sand during a storm snapping pictures."

"How on earth did you get a rainbow picture? The sky is so heavy with clouds."

"For a few seconds, the sky opened up and filled with light. The perfect conditions for a rainbow. The window of opportunity was short though. But I think I got some good shots." Ryder was about to show me his pictures when our first customer of the day walked through the door. It was Mayor Price.

My ever astute assistant, Ryder, knowing that I was not a fan of the man, stepped forward to help him. I subtly took hold of Ryder's arm to stop him. "I'll help Mayor Price," I said with forced enthusiasm. "If you don't mind, there are a few boxes in the back that need unpacking."

Ryder was rightfully confused, but he nodded and headed to the back room. Yesterday's journey to the past provided more questions than answers. I was anxious to know a little more about Mayor Price's long lost relative, Jane Price. It seemed she had left the treasurer's position rather abruptly. I hoped the mayor would have some insight into his family's story. I also hoped he'd consider telling me about it. I held out much less hope for the latter. Almost from the moment I'd arrived in town, Mayor Price had made no effort to hide his dislike of me. He seemed to consider it highly suspicious that a woman would walk away from a lucrative career in the city to open a flower shop in a small town. I was annoyed and hurt at first, but I had since come to grips with the fact that he just didn't care for me. It was also why I had no problem asking him a few personal questions. It wasn't like we had a friendship to protect.

I could always count on several givens when I met face to face with Mayor Price. The first being that I could expect a grumpy expression on his round face. I could expect his face to darken some with irritation. And I could expect his fluffy moustache to be badly trimmed. It was always longer on one side or the other. This morning it was leaning to the left.

I put on my brightest smile. "How can I help you, Mayor Price? We have some beautiful Valentine's bouquets available." I steered him toward the window where the examples were displayed.

He glowered at the empty bird perch. I was suddenly thankful for this morning's rainstorm and my bird's aversion to water.

"Did you finally get rid of that blasted menace of a bird?" he asked gruffly.

"Why, Mayor Price, that would be like asking me if I finally got rid of a beloved member of my family." My response caused his crooked moustache to rock back and forth over his straight line mouth.

"Wild animals are best left in the wild."

"Of course," I said working hard to hide the mocking in my tone. "Now which bouquet would you like to order?" I decided to skip Ryder's cute explanation of each arrangement. Somehow, Mayor Price didn't seem the type who would find humor in it.

"My wife likes lilies. Roses make her sneeze."

"Then she won't like any of these. I'll arrange a beautiful bouquet of lilies." We walked back to the island so I could write up the order. I'd hoped for an opportunity or easy segue into a conversation about his late relatives, but our interaction was so stiff and awkward, it just didn't happen.

I pointed to the spinning carousel of cards. "A gift card is free with the bouquet, so if you'd like to pick one and fill it out, I'll include it in the flowers." I placed the box of colored pens we provided for card signing on the counter.

He pulled out the first card he saw on the rack and opened it to sign. It was obvious that unlike most of the townsfolk who came in to buy flowers, Mayor Price wanted no small talk. I was going to be sorely disappointed in myself if he walked out and I didn't at least inquire about Jane Price.

I finished writing up the order and pretended to be distracted by the pitter patter of rain on the sidewalk outside the store. "I guess they aren't going to be taking any pictures this morning up on Maple Hill. It seems I had something to do with the Georgio's company choosing our quaint town and Hawksworth Manor for a marketing location." I paused in case he wanted to take the time to thank me. I had no doubt that Jacob paid a nice price for access to the site. No thank you came. He continued to write on the card, which was surprising because he seemed very much the *Happy Valentine's Day, Sincerely, Harlan* type.

"I'm embarrassed to say I'm sort of obsessed with that old place," I continued in a frilly tone. "I've spent countless hours poring over hundred-year-old newspaper articles at the library." A bit of an over-exaggeration but it seemed appropriate for the setting, and it helped me set up my inquiry.

Mayor Price responded with a low grunt. He continued writing his sentiment. It seemed I was going to be the cause of Mrs. Price receiving a lengthy, romantic message.

I forged ahead. "In fact, I came across a very debonair picture of Mayor Harvard Price on the front page of the Chesterton Gazette."

I'd finally gotten his attention. His left leaning moustache shifted back and forth as he looked up at me. "Why were you looking up my great-grandfather?" Apparently, everything I did was worthy of his suspicion.

"I wasn't. I was looking for articles about the Hawksworth Manor, and I saw an interesting looking man sitting behind a desk with a young woman standing next to him holding the town's treasury ledger. I had no idea who the people were until I read the picture caption. Your family has quite a legacy here in

Port Danby." My last comment seemed to soften his expression some.

His shoulders pushed back proudly. "A Price has been mayor of this town since 1900."

"And it seems they've held other positions of esteem as well. I noticed the woman in the picture was Jane Price, the town treasurer. She must have been your great aunt."

His face crinkled some at the mention of the name, and the earlier softening disappeared completely. His rocking horse moustache went into overdrive. "She was only my grandfather's half sister, and she left Port Danby at an early age."

"Why is that?"

He pushed the card abruptly toward me. "Should I pay now or when I pick it up?" he barked. It seemed I'd asked one question too many.

"That's up to you, Mayor Price."

"I'll pay when I pick it up." He walked out as if flames were chasing his heels.

CHAPTER 13

*L*ola walked into the store holding a manila folder in her hand. She paced the floor of the shop as I finished helping a customer with her order. As the customer asked a string of questions, Lola's impatient eye rolls got more dramatic. The woman was finally satisfied that she'd be able to properly care for her tray of herbs. She paid and Ryder came out from the backroom to carry the plants to her car.

Lola hadn't bothered to pull on a coat or grab an umbrella for her trip across the street. Her Rolling Stones t-shirt was spotted with raindrops. She hopped up on the stool, her usual perch when she visited. Her shoulders tensed some as Ryder stepped back into the shop, but she didn't turn back to say hello or acknowledge him. He took that as his cue to return to the back room.

Lola snuck a peek at him walking away.

I cleared my throat to assure her I'd caught the lingering look. She shrugged hard enough that drops of water fell from her hair onto the folder she'd placed down in front of her. She wiped the drops away. "Since my dear friend can't find the time to stop by my shop to look at some interesting pictures, I decided to brave the inclement weather and bring the pictures to her."

"I'm sorry, Lola. I forgot all about the pictures. The truth is, I've been so busy, and Hazel has dropped by numerous times to chat, taking up all my spare time."

"Yes, she sort of buzzes around like a bumble bee."

I laughed. "Actually, more like a hummingbird. I think she just misses having me to talk to. It's actually kind of nice to know at least one person missed me after I left Georgio's." I walked around to sit on the stool next to hers. "But there are no more customers, so you have my undivided attention."

"For a change," she quipped under her breath. She pulled the folder closer. "Anyhow, I was searching through those attic relics my parents picked up on the east coast, and I came across a box that had mostly useless stuff, a silver plated hair brush that had no bristles left, a few hand embroidered handkerchiefs that were too stained to save and a small stack of pictures that were tied up with a frayed red ribbon. Most of them were just of people out on a lawn playing croquet in front of a big brick house, but a few of them were very unusual."

Lola pulled a photo out of the folder. A woman wearing an enormous round skirt beneath a short bodice with drop sleeves and an ornate yolk, all typical of the mid nineteenth century, stood on the front porch of a large brick house. Something about her face looked tight. She might have been upset or trying hard to hold back a smile. It was hard to tell.

"It's a very nice picture, Lola. Very clear, considering the age."

Lola lifted it higher. "Look closer. I didn't bring it just to show you a severe looking woman in a cumbersome dress. There's something unusual about the picture."

I adjusted my glasses and lifted the image closer.

"Look directly to her left. What do you see?"

My gaze shifted away from the woman, the focal point of the

picture. The deep red brick of the facade looked slate gray in the photo. That dark color provided a stark background contrast for the milky white smear of haze right next to the woman. "I see something cloudy next to her. Maybe the photographer messed up on the development of the film?"

"That was my first guess, but stare at the haze a little longer. Block out the rest of the picture and look just at the milky smear on the porch."

I honed in on the fuzzy blur next to the woman. As I blotted out the surroundings and focused on the haze, a figure seemed to appear. A pair of tall dark boots stretched up to what looked like fawn colored breeches. My gaze traveled up along a waistcoat and cravat and stopped at a pair of intense dark eyes looking directly into mine. "Holy moly," I sucked in a sharp breath and dropped the picture.

"You see him too." Lola was slightly pale from my reaction. "I was almost hoping it was just my imagination, but if you see—"

"A man dressed in tall boots, breeches and a waistcoat." I was still trying to catch my breath.

"And a roguish smile?" she added.

"And a dark, intense gaze." I pulled my hand away from my chest, a reflex caused by the sudden loss of breath. I picked up the picture. The bell on the door clanged, startling me. The photo floated out of my fingers again.

"Your bestie is back," Lola muttered under her breath. She quickly swept up the pictures and shoved them into her folder. "Well, thank you, Pink, for your professional opinion on these-these advertising flyers. I'll talk to you more about them later." Lola winked and jumped off the stool, leaving me still stunned and even a touch dizzy.

Hazel's cheeks were puffed with an ear to ear grin as she nodded politely at Lola, who whisked past her like she was on roller blades. It was still cold and wet, but Hazel was apparently so fond of the new sweater from the Mod Frock, she'd decided not to cover it with more suitable wet weather clothing.

Hazel climbed up on the stool that Lola had just vacated and rested her hands on the edge of the counter. "I hope I didn't interrupt anything. I just had to get away from the site." She burst right into her rant rather than wait to find out if she had interrupted something. Which she had, only I wasn't exactly sure what it was that she'd disrupted. The logical side of my mind was working on some kind of camera manipulation or double exposure theory.

"Everyone is bored and grumpy up at the site. I could swear that big old mansion is sick and tired of us too. It looks even more dejected than ever. Autumn and Jasper decided to do a spa day inside Jasper's trailer. Jacob and Lydia were hibernating in their trailers. So I hightailed it out of there. Do you know where the ambulance is heading?"

Sirens sounded in the distance. With my head still dazed from the eerie photograph, it took me a second to answer Hazel's question.

I walked to the window. "I can't see them, but they seem to be north of town. I'm sure this rain has caused some nasty fender bender or something."

I walked back to the counter. "I've got to arrange some flowers for a birthday party, Hazel. Maybe we can meet for lunch today," I added, not wanting to hurt her feelings for trying to hurry her out.

"Yes, that would be wonderful."

A ray of sunlight landed on the side of my face. Fingers of warmth were starting to stream through the front windows. "Although, it looks like the sun will be out soon. Clouds roll out of the port almost as quickly as they roll in. I suppose all of you might have to work this afternoon since you've had the morning off."

Hazel smiled as if she hadn't heard a word I said.

"Hazel?"

"Hmm, oh sorry. Those sirens just had me distracted. There

seems to be so many of them." She plastered on a tight smile. "I'll leave you to your work then and see you at lunch."

"Sounds good."

Hazel hurried out quickly. It seemed I might have upset her, but I'd make it up to her later.

I shook off the worry that I'd hurt Hazel's feelings and started work on my flower arrangements. I'd pushed the sound of the sirens out of my head until Ryder stepped out from the back. "Sounds like there must have been a big accident."

He was right. Multiple sirens echoed through town. I walked to the window again and reached it just as Detective Briggs sped up Harbor Lane. He had placed the portable light on top of his undercover car. From my shop window, I could only see to the end of Harbor Lane where it turned right onto Myrtle Place or left onto Culpepper Road. His car veered right.

If Detective Briggs' car was heading to the right it meant something had happened near my home. I turned to Ryder. "I'm going up to my house. I want to make sure nothing has happened to any of my neighbors."

"I'll hold down the fort," Ryder said. "Let me know what's up," he called as I hurried out the door.

CHAPTER 14

$\mathcal{B}$y the time I turned onto Myrtle Place, Briggs' car was speeding past Loveland Terrace and heading up Maple Hill. As relieved as I was that the emergency wasn't on my street, I was equally worried that someone up at the photo shoot had been hurt. My mind briefly drifted to the worrisome notion that Jacob's cold had turned far worse. But Detective Briggs was rarely called for an illness or heart attack. It had to be something far more grave than a case of pneumonia or rigorous case of the flu.

Officer Chinmoor had parked his squad car horizontally across Maple Hill, giving just enough room for only the emergency vehicles to pass. Chinmoor stood guard, not allowing the many curious spectators who had already climbed the hill on foot to get closer to the Hawksworth Manor. I made a last second decision to park in my driveway and walk up the hill on foot. The rain had stopped, and it seemed sunshine was not far off.

Dash's tall blond head stood up above the others who had gathered. With spring and fair weather approaching soon, Dash had been extra busy at the marina where his job was to tune up and fix boat engines. But the rain had given him the morning off and some much needed time to work on his house. It seemed the symphony of sirens had pulled him from his kitchen remodel project.

Dash waved me over. My heart was pounding, not so much from the uphill hike but from the prospect that someone I knew had been hurt . . . or worse.

I reached him, and my nerves caused me to fire off a barrage of questions rather than allow Dash to tell me what he knew. "Is it an injury? Is it those treacherous stairs in the house? I just knew someone would go inside to explore. Who is it? Who got hurt?"

"Whoa, slow down there, Lacey. You're rattling off way more questions than I have answers for." He'd said it lightly, but it took him only another second of looking at my fretful expression to change his tone. He put a supportive arm around my shoulder. "That's right. These are people you know. I'm sorry for sounding so cheerful."

"It's all right. I came at you like a three-year-old with a million questions. What's going on? Can you tell?"

He paused.

"Don't worry, Dash. I'm a big girl. I can handle it."

He lowered his arm. "I don't know much of anything. I walked up here after the third or fourth siren screamed past. Chinmoor was already here, playing sentry and keeping everyone else back. What I can tell you is that the paramedics had all their equipment piled on a gurney. They rolled it up to that third trailer in the line of vehicles. The Mayfield fire truck had gotten to the scene first, along with a few of their squad cars. The police and firemen were standing at the bottom of the trailer steps. They had a conversation with the paramedics. The paramedics never went inside. Briggs rolled up just minutes later. He went right inside the trailer with a few of the officers close at his heels."

My limbs felt heavy with dread. The last few statements

assured me that something terrible had happened, that the person inside the trailer was dead.

"I've got to find out what's going on, Dash." I left him behind and elbowed my way to the front of the crowd. My eyes quickly scanned the scene, looking for familiar faces. Hazel, Lydia and Autumn were standing in front of the caterer's truck in a supportive circle, with arms around each other. That took all three of them off my worry list. I was sure if I could get Hazel's attention, she'd head over and fill me in, but she hadn't looked my direction. From their postures and the tissue clutched in Autumn's hand, it seemed my worst suspicions of a death were confirmed. Lydia's ankle length, flowing sweater blocked whoever was standing at the center of the circle. Whoever it was, they weren't taller than the three women in front, which meant Jacob was not there. Quick flashes of some of the more charming moments of our relationship passed through my mind, like a life passing before me. Only it wasn't my life, it was Jacob's. Or to be more precise, Jacob's life with me. I thought about the horrid tasting omelet he had cooked me one morning. It was so laden with salt, it made my eyes water. But I ate every bite because he had been so excited to make it for me. A long, supposed to be romantic cruise around the harbor where I ended up so seasick, he had to carry me back to the parking lot. Just as my eyes started to burn with the possibility that Jacob was the person in the trailer, his tall figure appeared in the corner of my eye. He hadn't taken the time to put on a coat as he trudged with heavy steps across the lot toward the others.

I was so relieved to see him, I burst through the crowd and took off at a run. Officer Chinmoor whistled and angrily shouted my name. His sound of alarm brought everyone's attention my direction. Before I could throw my arms around Jacob, Hazel intercepted the hug with one of her own.

"Oh, Lacey, it's just awful. I can't even believe it. Maybe that horrid house has evil spirits after all."

She was rambling and blubbering and I let her continue, without asking questions. I peered over her shoulder at Jacob. He looked stunned and pale and speechless. Hazel's parting from the group revealed that a highly distraught Alexander had been standing in the center of the group. It grew easier to deduce who the victim was.

Just then a deep voice, probably the best voice I could hear at a time of great distress, called my name.

"Miss Pinkerton."

Hazel released me, and I turned around. Detective Briggs was standing at the bottom of the trailer steps with his black winter coat buttoned up and his black fedora hat in hand. With my nerves frazzled and my emotions running high, he was such a welcome sight, a small, hard to define sound escaped me. I took a deep breath to gain control and walked over to him.

Briggs scrutinized my expression, obviously trying to read my emotional state. "I could use your assistance. However, if this is too close to home for you—"

"No," I said quickly and without thinking. I reminded myself that someone I knew would be laying dead in the trailer. I nodded. "If you need my assistance, I'm here for you." There was only one meaning behind my statement, but for a second we looked at each other as if there was a million other ways to interpret it. Sometimes Briggs and I were so busy we went weeks without even passing each other on the street, but whenever I was standing face to face with the man, all I could think was how much I'd missed seeing him.

It took me a second to collect my words. Under normal circumstances, (normal being a murder scene where I didn't know the victim) my feet would have been ready to spring into a happy dance at being asked to assist. But this was entirely different. Still, if I could help, then I wanted a chance.

"Please, yes, it will be difficult. But I can help you collect evidence if that's what you need."

Briggs nodded and turned to go back up the steps. I stopped him by placing my hand on his arm. "Is it Jasper Edmonton?"

"Yes, it is."

I took my hand away to let him know I was ready. I immediately chastised myself for all the mean and disparaging things I'd ever said or thought about Jasper. He was far too young to have such a terrible end.

CHAPTER 15

$\mathcal{T}$he dizzying mix of scents as we stepped into the eight by twenty foot trailer caught me off guard. Briggs took my hesitation as not wanting to see the body. He took hold of my elbow to steady me.

"We can turn back around," he said quietly.

"No, it's the mix of fragrances inside this small space. I hadn't prepared myself. I'm fine."

I'd also been unprepared to see Jasper, lifeless and still, with his extremely handsome face covered in a dark pink clay mask. Large circles framed his eyes and mouth, giving him a frightening, macabre look.

After the proven success of the ad campaign featuring Jasper and Autumn, the modeling agency had asked for more perks for their models. By the third shoot, Georgio's had sprung for a personal, private traveling trailer for each model. Jasper had his trailer decorated in expensive furniture, including the sumptuous, richly upholstered sofa where his limp body lay. One arm hung off the sofa like a doll's arm and his mouth was slack. There were a few bite marks on his bottom lip. The only true detail that showed just how spectacular Jasper looked when he was alive were his rich, dark eyelashes, which now, closed in death gave him a boyish quality.

"Nothing has been touched yet," Briggs noted. "I'm waiting for the coroner." He pointed out a pillow, a contrasting accent pillow from the sofa. It was smeared with the pink clay from Jasper's facial mask. "It seems the victim was taking a nap when someone smothered him with a pillow. That most likely limits our field of suspects to someone who was strong enough to hold a pillow down over a young, well-built man once he woke up."

"Was it definitely murder?" I was half-heartedly still hoping it wasn't because murder would most likely indicate one of the other people I knew from Georgio's. But who?

"I'll know more once Nate arrives to inspect the body, but all indications are it was murder by suffocation." Briggs pulled out his notebook, his nod to the old-fashioned implements of good detective work, something I'd always found charming. Somehow, he just wouldn't be as fun to watch if he was inputting everything on a tablet. "The body was discovered by Alexander Nettles. He's the location scout for the crew."

"Yes, I know. I know all of them."

"I figured as much. That's why I hesitated to ask for your help. But if you wouldn't mind, Miss Pinkerton." He handed me a pair of latex gloves.

I pulled them on and circled around to the pillow. If someone had smothered poor Jasper, then they could have left certain scents on the murder weapon or, in this case, murder pillow. It was somehow worse to think a successful, young life had been snuffed out by an accent pillow.

If I touched the pillow, I needed to return it to the same place and position. I'd been on a few cases with Detective Briggs, something that usually thrilled me. I loved unraveling a good mystery, but this one was going to be much harder than normal. I could only imagine what my ex-coworkers were going through at the moment.

I knelt down to the floor where the pillow was wedged between the sofa and the coffee table. The coffee table, a small polished-wood oval was strewn with wet washcloths and the empty clay mask jar. Hazel had mentioned that Jasper and Autumn were going to use the free morning for a spa day.

I lowered my face to the pillow. The pink clay mask had a strong aroma of rosehip and something citrus, lemon possibly. I carefully lifted it up and ran my nose along the back side of the pillow. I stopped at the end of the fabric, stunned and feeling a little sick to my stomach.

I pushed the pillow closer. The strong fragrance of the mask on the pillow and on Jasper's face nearly hid the faint odor on the back of the pillow. I needed to be sure. I took a deep whiff again. My stomach tightened more. It couldn't be. It was too incredible to consider. There were two distinct odors on the back of the pillow, and I knew both smells well.

"Miss Pinkerton," Briggs' deep voice cascaded down over me, snapping me out of my moment of shock. "Miss Pinkerton, do you smell something? Something that could be evidence?"

I was too speechless and thick throated to answer. I peered up at him and nodded.

I placed the pillow back down in the same position. Something red and white caught my eye. I leaned down and pulled a single sock out from under the couch. It was not a man's sock. I took a quick whiff of it. It smelled of nail lacquer and Georgio's perfume. It most likely belonged to Autumn. I placed it back in the same spot. "You'll want to collect the sock as well. I don't think it belongs to the victim."

"And the smell on the pillow?" he asked, naturally. Only I wished that he hadn't. I wished the pillow hadn't been there at all.

Briggs was quite adept at reading my expressions. He lowered his hand for me to take. "You look as if you need some air."

I still had the gloves on. Even though I was not particularly in a solid state of mind, I pulled them off before placing my hand in his. It seemed the last time he'd proffered me a gallant hand up, I was wearing thick winter gloves. It had been more than a little disappointing. His hand was strong with slightly callused palms as his fingers wrapped around mine. His firm grasp was exactly what I needed at that moment because I was feeling more than a little shaky from head to toe.

He led me to the door. "I haven't done a thorough nose search of the scene yet," I noted.

"That's all right. You look pale and not yourself." He opened the door. Nate Blankenship, the local coroner, pulled up in his van as we stepped outside. The fresh air felt good on my face.

"We'll let Nate do his thing while you and I talk." Briggs turned to me before we walked down. "Because my detective senses tell me you might have a hunch about our murder suspect."

I looked around and found everyone, all of my ex-coworkers and my ex-fiancé huddled together across the way. My heart sank into my stomach and another wave of nausea washed over me.

I took a deep breath and looked back at Briggs. "Yes, I do."

CHAPTER 16

*B*riggs walked me down the steps and left my side for a few minutes to fill Nate Blankenship in on the murder scene. Hazel saw me standing alone and scurried across the rain soaked ground.

She grabbed my arm and held it tightly. She seemed to be holding it together pretty well considering the circumstances. But then Hazel was almost always the one to keep calm when problems arose at Georgio's.

"Lacey, we saw that detective walk you inside Jasper's trailer." She pressed her hand to her lips to stifle a cry. "I guess everything I've read is true. You are part of the investigative team down here in Port Danby. I sure hope you can find the monster who did this to poor Jasper. The rest of us are just destroyed. It's so terrible that it's hard to believe any of this is real. I keep expecting to wake up from a bad dream."

I looked past her to the others. They all looked pale and stunned by the nightmarish reality that one of their own had been murdered. Even Jacob, I noted.

"How is Jacob taking it?" My voice wavered as I spoke.

Hazel looked back at him. She had finally pulled on a proper winter coat over the mod sweater. "He's taking it just as hard as the rest of us. I see you still hold a special place in your heart for him."

"Why would you say that?" I asked abruptly.

Hazel immediately scrambled to apologize. "I didn't mean anything by it. It's just that you singled him out just now." She squeezed my arm. "Obviously, we're all just a little on edge. And to realize that a cold-blooded murderer is lurking somewhere around your town must be very disconcerting to you."

I didn't have the heart to tell her that I suspected the murderer might be closer than she imagined.

Briggs returned to where I was standing.

"Detective Briggs, this is Hazel Bancroft. She is an administrative assistant who pretty much runs the whole company while no one is looking." I managed to work up a friendly wink at Hazel. She seemed more than pleased with my compliment.

Briggs pulled out his notepad to write down her name.

Hazel stretched her neck up to try and look at the notepad. "What are you writing down?" she asked.

"Just your name. I'll be taking a statement from everyone who worked with Mr. Edmonton. But if you wouldn't mind, right now I need to talk to Miss Pinkerton alone."

Hazel seemed reluctant to leave my side. "Go on, Hazel. I'll talk to you later."

She nodded. "Nice meeting you, Detective Briggs. And of course, if there's anything you need, you just have to ask." We watched as Hazel hurried back to the others. Jacob had turned his focus away from his employees and on to his ex-employee. Our gazes caught for a fleeting second before Briggs led me to a more secluded place between the trailers.

"That tall man, that's Jacob Georgio, the owner of Georgio's?" Briggs asked.

"Yes, that's him."

"And he—you and him—he was your—"

"We were once engaged if that's the question you're trying to formulate."

"Yes." He looked properly embarrassed about his prying question. He pulled out his notepad to move on from the topic. "It seemed you smelled something on the pillow that was possibly used to smother the victim."

"Possibly?" I asked enthusiastically. "So it's possible something else was used? It's possible the pillow had nothing to do with the murder?"

His dark brow arched. "I wouldn't use the word *possible*. The same clay mask that was on the victim's face was on the pillow. And the pillow was sitting right next to the couch. I would say it's highly likely that it was used by the perpetrator. Just like I'd say it's highly likely that you smelled something significant on that pillow."

I peered at him questioningly.

"Your face blanched and you looked very distressed right after you smelled the pillow."

I pulled my coat closer around me, for no other reason except it made me feel better. "I smelled a certain cologne on the back of the pillow. It's a special blend of cedarwood and cypress with a bergamot oil twist."

Briggs blinked those annoyingly attractive eyelashes at me as he waited for me to elaborate. I knew the ingredients meant nothing to him, but they meant a great deal to me.

"It's a very unique blend that the chemists created for one person. It's not on the market. Or at least not that I know of," I added. Obviously sensing my distress, he was being extra patient this morning. I took a deep breath. "The Georgio's chemists created the cologne for Jacob Georgio."

"Are you certain it's the same scent?"

I shrugged. I wanted to be anything but certain. "We were—we were together at the time. Jacob let me create the cologne because —" I had no idea just how difficult this would all be until I began saying everything out loud. "He wanted to be sure that I liked it."

Briggs' jaw did that little twitch thing that happened occasionally. I'd learned that it was his police detective way of hiding any emotion he was feeling. I'd theorized that his suppressed feelings had to come out somewhere and that the twitch was his release, his spout on the tea kettle.

He jostled himself out of whatever had taken over his thoughts and suddenly remembered he needed to write things down. He pulled out his notepad and flipped it to a clean page. He pressed his pen to the paper but looked back up at me before writing. "So you created the scent. You recognize it as the custom fragrance that only Jacob Georgio wears?"

It felt as if my head was filled with cement as I nodded. "But you'll have it analyzed, right? I mean my nose could be wrong."

His left brow shifted up to show doubt on that last statement. He was right. My nose was always pretty spot on. Darn my hyperosmia. And then, I silently reminded myself, there was the second aroma on the pillow. One that was even easier to discern than the cologne. "Clove cigarettes," I said quietly as he wrote his notes.

Briggs looked up. "Clove cigarettes? You smelled that too?"

"Yes. On the pillow. They have a very distinctive odor and if a person smokes one, it permeates their clothes, just like a tobacco cigarette."

"Is it possible the deceased smoked them?" he asked.

I shook my head. "Not that I know of."

"Which of your coworkers smoked clove cigarettes?" He readied his pen as if waiting for a list. I wished there had been a list to give.

"Jacob is the only person I know who smokes clove cigarettes."

Briggs wrote the name down but didn't look up this time. He

avoided eye contact completely. He knew this was extremely diffi-cult for me. He took his time finishing his notes and then closed the pad and stuck it back in his coat pocket.

"I've known Jacob a long time. He just isn't capable of murder. I just thought I should add that." Unfortunately, saying it didn't help relieve the guilt I was feeling.

Briggs finally looked at me, but there was a long, significant pause before he spoke. "Thank you for your help with this, Lacey." He almost never called me Lacey. "I'll let you go. I'm sure you have a busy day ahead of you. As do I."

CHAPTER 17

I knew I wasn't going to be able to just slip away. Everyone stood around looking dazed, confused and distraught. Autumn was clutching a paper bag to her face, apparently staving off another fit of hyperventilation, and Lydia stood with Alexander, both with faces so pale, they looked close to throwing up. While the others were consoling each other, Hazel seemed to count on me for comfort. The moment Briggs left my side, she raced over and glued herself to me.

Jacob had wandered away from everyone else to make phone calls. This was going to be a big shock to the board members and everyone else back at the office.

Hazel and I watched him pacing back and forth in front of the manor, with his phone stuck to his ear. "I wouldn't want to be him right now," she said.

My face snapped her direction. "Why not? What have you heard?"

Hazel's lips rolled in and disappeared. She was rightly confused by my abrupt line of questioning. I was so on edge I hadn't thought before speaking. "Oh, you mean because he has to tell everyone back home." I shook my head. "I'm sorry. I'm just a little out of sorts about all of this."

Naturally, I hadn't mentioned one thing to anyone. My investigative work was strictly business. I had to keep my personal connections to the murder out of the way. It was going to be hard.

"I confess I know little about Jasper's life. Did he have a large family? A significant other?" I asked.

"As far as I know, he was living alone in his apartment in the city. I think his parents live somewhere in the Midwest, but from what Lydia has told me, they were estranged. He hadn't spoken to them since he was a teenager."

"That's always so hard for me to fathom, not speaking to my parents. After I dropped out of medical school and then gave up my nice position at Georgio's, my parents were still speaking to me. I'm pretty sure there is nothing else I can do to disappoint them, so our relationship is solid."

"Same here. And my parents are my landlords. Talk about putting a strain on the relationship."

"I bet they'll miss you a lot when you move."

"Move?" she asked.

"When you take the position at Tremaine's Fashion House."

"Oh yes." She laughed lightly. "With all that's happened, I nearly forgot about my new job. No wonder Jacob always calls me a scatterbrain."

"He does? Hazel, if there's one person I would never refer to as a scatterbrain, it's you. He takes you too much for granted. I assure you, he'll notice when you're gone."

"I think so too." Activity around the trailer had ramped up, which meant they were likely to remove Jasper's body soon. "Do they know what happened to Jasper?" Hazel asked.

"I think so, but I'll have to wait and let Detective Briggs fill everyone in." Once he left my side, Briggs had disappeared inside the trailer. He had been in there for a long time collecting evidence.

Hazel and I were just about to join the others when Briggs appeared in the doorway of the trailer with Nate.

"Who is that man with the detective?" Hazel asked.

"That's the coroner. It looks like they're getting ready to move Jasper's body."

That statement shook Hazel. I regretted saying it so plainly. I kept an eye on the activity as I hugged her. Briggs' gaze swept the area. It landed on me for a brief moment. I could read his thoughts as if they were written across his forehead. It seemed I was getting more experienced at detective work. I knew exactly what he would do next.

Briggs walked down the steps and strode purposefully across the lot to Jacob. Jacob saw him approach and quickly finished up his phone call. I studied Jacob's reaction, trying to find some indication of guilt or worry on his face, but all I saw was the same pale, drawn look that the others were wearing.

Jacob's face changed some as Briggs spoke to him. Then he turned and led Detective Briggs toward his own trailer. This was it. Briggs would be looking for evidence that matched what I'd found in Jasper's trailer. And I was sure he'd find plenty, or at least enough to take Jacob in for questioning. None of this was making sense, and all of it had me feeling more than a little sick to my stomach. For once I wished I hadn't *dug my nose* into police business.

CHAPTER 18

nstead of Nevermore waking me with a claw sharpening session, he nudged me softly with his head. Since he slept on the end of my bed, he knew I'd had a rough night. I had probably burned more calories from tossing and turning in my bed than I'd burned all day at work.

I lifted my hand to rub Nevermore's head. My arm was heavy along with the rest of my limbs. But my heart was heaviest of all. I had finally dragged myself away from the depressing scene at Hawksworth Manor a few minutes after the coroner's van had gone down the hill. Alexander and Autumn were holding each other up as we watched Nate drive his van past, slowly and respectfully, much like the Hearst in a funeral procession. The ensuing sobs and hugs stopped abruptly though when Detective Briggs walked Jacob Georgio to the police car. Their boss was being taken in for questioning. Fortunately, none of them knew that I was partly to blame for that. I'd spent the rest of the work day, totally distracted. Ryder insisted I go home early. Which I did. I spent the rest of the afternoon huddled in my house with my two companions, Kingston and Nevermore. It was selfish, but I was relieved not to have to talk to anyone else for the rest of the day.

Nevermore nudged me once more for good measure and jumped down from the bed. I pushed off the covers and sat up. It felt as if I'd just finished a marathon instead of a night of sleep. I'd spent a good deal of the restless night hours trying to comprehend the possibility that Jacob was a cold-blooded murderer. But no matter what line of thinking I took, I couldn't come to that conclusion. The one question that kept popping up was what motive did Jacob have? Jasper was somewhat demanding and spoiled, but he was also an asset to the company. Sales and stocks went through the roof after Autumn and Jasper became the faces of Georgio's Perfume. As much as I had always wanted to take some of the credit for the perfumes, in the back of my mind I always knew that the reality was most people couldn't smell the subtle differences in the perfumes. Advertisements boasting that gorgeous, romantic people like Autumn and Jasper used Georgio's Perfume did much more to persuade people to buy the perfume than my microscopic tweaks to the formula.

I pulled on my robe and slippers and headed down the hallway to Kingston's cage. A low-flying helicopter rattled the house as I pulled off the cage cover. Kingston flapped in alarm, sending a few downy black feathers from the cage. They stuck to my slippers.

A knock followed the buzz of the helicopter. I sighed, sure it was Hazel. I was glad to be there for her, but at the same time, I'd forgotten how needy she could be. I'd basically ignored my Port Danby friends because Hazel had taken up so much of my spare time.

I walked to the door. Hazel was holding a tissue in her hand. She quickly wiped her nose and shoved it into her coat pocket. "I'm sorry. I just can't seem to stop crying." She pushed past me. "Everything is such a mess, and now they've got Jacob in custody."

I shut the door. "They do?"

"Well, he's at the police station waiting for his lawyer to join him before he answers any more questions. Remember Baxter Redmond, his lawyer? He's on his way. I personally don't think he's the right lawyer for a murder charge."

"Wait, what charge? Has Jacob been charged?"

Hazel looked baffled. "Isn't that what it means when they take someone in for questioning?"

"No, not necessarily. And what motive would Jacob have? None of this makes sense."

Hazel walked right into my small living room and took off her coat. Apparently, she was staying for breakfast. "Well, between you and me, I think this is all Lydia's fault," she said as she looked around for a place to put her coat. I took it from her and hung it next to mine.

"Lydia? Why do you think that?"

"After we each had our private chat with the detective, Lydia and I compared notes. Apparently, she blabbed all kinds of office gossip to the man." Hazel sat with a flourish on the couch. She'd come to my door in tears, but she seemed to have gotten over the emotional moment quickly. "Lydia told him that Jacob and Autumn had been dating these past six month and that lately, Autumn and Jasper had been doing some heavy flirting. She let him know that they were once a couple as well." Hazel lifted her nose in the air for a whiff. "I hate to be a bother, but do have any coffee? With everything that's going on the catering crew basically threw up their hands in strike and told us to get our own coffee and breakfast."

"I was just going to make a pot."

Hazel followed me into the kitchen. "Poor Jacob," she lamented as she watched me fill the pot. "Lydia should have kept her mouth shut. There was no reason for her to bring up any of the stuff she said, and I told her as much. Now she's not talking to me."

"Maybe Lydia just thought it was the right thing to mention." I hoped no one would ever find out about the evidence I'd found but something told me those hopes would be dashed soon enough.

"I think her decision to say something was self serving. She's so angry at all of them, Jacob and the other board members. And the models, for that matter." Hazel leaned down to pat Nevermore on the head. My cat was waiting for breakfast and therefore, had little interest in a pat. I reached into the cupboard for a can of cat food.

Hazel's last comment had pricked my amateur detective ears. "Why is Lydia angry?"

"She found out that Autumn and Jasper were making three times what she was making, and when she asked for a raise, Jacob had to turn her down. In his defense, he did take it to the board for a vote. But I know she was still mad as heck about it. She said once her contract with Georgio's was up, she was going to pack up her cameras and tripod and head for fairer skies."

"Maybe you could find her a position at Tremaine's," I suggested as I pulled the creamer out of the refrigerator.

"Yes maybe."

Another low flying helicopter rattled the house. This time it didn't faze Kingston.

"Ugh," Hazel grunted, "the locusts are already swarming the town, anxious to get a story."

"Locusts? The media? That was fast."

"The second news of Jasper's passing went up on his Facebook page, the story was everywhere. People didn't know him by name, but they certainly knew him as that hot looking man in the Georgio's Perfume ad. And since he was murdered, well, that's extra big news."

"See, and that makes the entire notion of Jacob killing off his model even more silly," I said more to myself than to Hazel. "This will be horrible publicity for the company. Why would Jacob sabotage his own company's reputation?"

Hazel shrugged. "For love?"

I shook my head. "Like I said before, none of this makes sense." I needed to go to the station and talk to Briggs. The motive was thin at best, and besides his freedom, Jacob had everything to lose from Jasper's murder. Autumn was a beautiful woman, but I just couldn't see Jacob throwing away everything to keep her. But then maybe I was just being a jealous ex. I let my mind mull that possibility for a moment. No, that was ridiculous. I'd barely given the man a moment's thought since . . . well, since he walked into my new hometown.

I poured Hazel some coffee.

"I'm going to get dressed, Hazel. I have to get to the shop, but I need to make a few stops first."

"Darn, I was hoping we could have breakfast. It looks like we're all going to be stuck here for the rest of the week until this horrible nightmare is sorted out."

"I'm afraid I'm going to have to take a rain check on breakfast."

CHAPTER 19

I had a good hour before I needed to open the shop. It gave me just enough time to walk down to the station and see Briggs. Or so I thought until I came up against a wall of news reporters and cameras. I suppose it was naive of me to have thought this murder would have gone unnoticed by the public.

Officer Chinmoor had been given the unenviable job of keeping the press back and warning them not to block pedestrians on the sidewalk. His warning resulted in a few of the camera men moving their unwieldy equipment off the walkway. I pushed through at the first sign of an opening.

Officer Chinmoor didn't recognize me in my coat and scarf. He put up his hand to stop me from entering the station. "Oh, Miss Pinkerton," he said, "it's you. Is Detective Briggs expecting you?"

"Yes." I hated lying but decided this was one of those necessary white lies. A man's whole life was at stake.

Chinmoor pushed open the door. I hurried inside so he could pull it shut behind me before a pushy reporter squeezed through.

Hilda, the retired police woman who ran the front desk in Port

Danby's police station, looked as frazzled as Officer Chinmoor as she poked her head up to see who had entered.

"Oh, hello, Lacey," she sighed. "Can you believe this hullabaloo?" She pushed from her chair and dropped her voice. "Detective Briggs is so angry about the chaos out on the sidewalk. You know he hates to have things interfere with his investigation, and hoards of news crews certainly does that. There were even news helicopters circling the town so low they were setting off car alarms and causing every dog in the neighborhood to howl."

"Yes, they made my whole house shake." I glanced past the counter to Briggs' office. His door was shut. "I hate to ask, Hilda, but do you think I could have a quick word with him? That is, if he isn't angry like a bear right now."

Hilda laughed. "Let me check." She knocked and went into Briggs' office. She emerged a few seconds later and walked to the buzzer to let me in. "Enter at your own risk," she whispered as I walked past.

Detective Briggs was sitting behind his desk, writing something on a report form as I walked in. Normally he would look up from his task and offer me a smile, but today he kept on writing. I walked to the chair in front of his desk and sat down.

He wrote a few more words and put down the pen before finally lifting his face. "Miss Pinkerton, I want to thank you again for your assistance yesterday with the Edmonton murder case." There was nothing I disliked more than Briggs talking to me in a formal, all-business manner. We'd spent far too much time together for such a starched conversation. I decided to ignore his manner and jumped right into my speech.

"I'm not entirely sure Jacob should be sitting here based solely on my assumptions that the odors on the pillow were from his cologne and clove cigarettes. There is a very good chance that I'm wrong."

His jaw shifted ever so slightly. "So you think your nose, the same nose that smelled the faintest scent of fresh cut lumber on a victim in the middle of a fishing pier in the dead of a winter storm mis-smelled?"

"For the record, I don't think mis-smelled is an actual term, and when you put it that way, it does sound as if I'm grasping at straws." It seemed the ice had been broken. His expression softened, and the stiffness in his shoulders melted.

I sat forward. "None of it makes sense. You've no doubt noticed, as Hilda called it, the hullabaloo out front. And I do think that word should come back in style. It's so much fun to say."

"I prefer brouhaha, but continue." Briggs leaned back and rested an arm on his chair, his silent gesture to let me know he was listening with an open mind. The pressure was on me to make a good case, but in truth I didn't have much.

"Jacob would never do anything that would shroud his family's company in bad publicity. Especially nothing so horrid as a murder."

"They say any publicity is good publicity. Just look at all the free advertisement he's getting this morning."

"While that is partially true, I hardly think killing off the much-adored model, who represents romance and passion for the company, is going to go over well with his customers. Jasper was arrogant and smug, but he had a huge fan base. There just wouldn't be any motive at all for Jacob to kill him."

"Except for the good old stand-by motive of jealousy." Briggs sat forward again and touched his notepad. "I had more than one of his employees tell me that Jacob was unhappy because Autumn and Jasper had been especially playful during the photograph sessions. Apparently, the two models had a relationship at one point in time."

"And what did Autumn, the female model, have to say? Because, frankly, I saw a photo shoot, and it seemed pretty obvious that she was just playing a game, trying to make Jacob jealous. Only I think

Jacob is a bit past the game playing stage in his life." I thought I was doing a good job making my case, but my words only seemed to make his shoulders stiffen again. I could see that formal wall going up between us.

He opened his notepad. "I didn't realize you were a witness. I should have interviewed you too, it seems." He wrote a few things down. "So you saw the flirtations between the two models and your ex—" He cleared his throat. "Your ex-boss was there to witness it too?"

I was thrown off by my sudden drop into the role of witness. I scooted on the chair to straighten my posture and regain my confidence. "Yes, I was there the previous morning. I'd followed Kingston up to the site. He flew up there to see what the—brouhaha was about." I winked at him. "Kingston knows that where there are people there are crumbs. But I digress. I walked up there to make sure Kingston was behaving himself and to say hello to all my old friends. Lydia, the photographer, was shooting pictures of Jasper and Autumn. They seemed to be having a good time with it. But Jacob was—"

"A good time? Could you elaborate?"

My earlier straight posture crumpled some. "I don't know, Detective Briggs. They were giggling and tickling each other. Jacob looked a bit like an angry rooster on the sidelines, but frankly, I think he was more miserable about his cold than about what was happening in front of the camera."

Briggs looked up at me. "You'll have to excuse me if I don't write the last part down because it's just conjecture on your part."

I stared at him, making sure to let him know I wasn't happy. Then I abruptly broke out of my role as witness. "Oh come on, Briggs, let's stop acting like we don't know each other. I'm not just some witness cold called off the street to answer questions. I'm the one who pointed out crucial evidence in a murder case. Just like I've done three times before."

"Evidence, it seems, you regret finding."

"Why did you just say it like that?"

"Like what?" It seemed we'd both broken out of formal character. "I'm just pointing out that you seem to regret having to implicate your ex—your ex-boss in a murder."

"Stop with that dramatic pause thing," I huffed. "You can say it, ex-fiancé. Jacob is my ex-fiancé. If you call my mom, she'll tell you how much she wished I'd stuck with him, even if he was wearing another woman's perfume on his shirt collar." I sat back. "Shoot. I'm just a chatty bird today, aren't I?" I scooted forward again. "Please let me talk to Jacob."

I put up my hand before he could say no.

"Ten minutes. Please. I'll be his one phone call, only it'll be face to face."

"He already had his phone call. It was to his father."

"So you've charged him?"

"Not officially, but everyone who gets pulled in for questioning always thinks they are owed that phone call. So I let them call. I'm waiting for confirmation that the cologne we found in Jacob's trailer is the scent on the pillow. And he won't answer any more questions without his lawyer present. Which, under the circumstances, is probably a smart move."

"James." I took a chance and used his real name. It seemed to soften his expression. "Please, just ten minutes."

A long silent pause followed. Then Briggs reached into his drawer and pulled out a set of keys. "Five minutes but the whole conversation will be considered off the record. Just a friend consoling a friend. You can keep whatever is said between you."

"Agreed."

CHAPTER 20

$\mathcal{J}$acob was sitting in the Port Danby interrogation room, which was really just a small room with a table, two chairs and a bench sitting beneath a window that looked out onto the street. A slightly crooked mini blind had been hung over the window. Several of the slats were missing, allowing a thin plank of sunlight into the room. There were no brutal looking interrogation lights hanging over the table like one might expect. In fact, the glass globe light that was positioned near the back of the room provided only a pale greenish glow.

Someone had brought Jacob one of Franki's three eggs and bacon breakfast plates and a coffee, but the food was mostly untouched. A box of tissue and pile of throat lozenges were sitting next to the plate of food.

Jacob was surprised to see me walk inside, but he was so sick and depressed, he hardly blinked an eye. I wasn't sure how much Briggs had told him about the scent on the pillow, but I was sure he'd mentioned his reasons for bringing Jacob in for questioning.

With that thought in my head, I sat gingerly on the chair across from him. I held my breath for a second, waiting to see if he'd tell me to get out. Instead, he plucked another throat lozenge from the pile and unwrapped it.

"I'm not mad at you, Lacey," he finally said. "I know you were just doing your job." He laughed. "Oh wait. It's not your job because you're not a damn forensic investigator."

"So that first mention of not being mad was sarcasm? Got it. And you're right, it's not my job. I've made myself and my nose useful in a few investigations, and the detective occasionally asks my opinion."

He shifted the lozenge back and forth in his mouth. "Is there a thing happening between you two?"

"Ugh, maybe this was a mistake."

"Right. Why are you here?"

"If you must know, I came here this morning to tell Briggs that contrary to evidence, I don't believe you had anything to do with Jasper's murder." Right then, loud voices on the sidewalk vibrated the window.

"What a Podunk little town. How do you keep your sanity around here? Look at this silly interrogation room."

"If you'd prefer to be sitting in between four cement walls with a one way window and painfully bright lights overhead, maybe you could request a harsher environment. But I think the breakfast, tissue and lozenges would be forbidden in a city police station." I sat forward feeling slightly sick that I'd be spending my five minutes on defense. "Jacob, I know you don't feel well and the situation seems dire at the moment, but stop being such a grump and talk to me. It's just you and me off the record. I don't work for the police."

His brow arched, and rightfully so.

"All right. I occasionally lend them my nose to sniff out clues, but this is just you and me talking. Where were you during the murder? Do you have any possible alibi?"

"Only if the bed in my trailer can talk. I felt awful. When the rain started to fall and Lydia called off the shoot, I trudged back to my trailer alone. I took some cold medicine, and I climbed into bed. I didn't wake up until I heard Alexander yelling that something was wrong with Jasper."

"Is that all you remember?" I'd been so thrown off by finding evidence that pointed to Jacob that I hadn't asked Briggs any of the usual details.

"Yes." Jacob put both elbows on the table and rested his forehead against the palms of his hands. "I didn't kill him," he muttered and then sat back. "I didn't kill him. Jasper was a pain, but he was pure gold when it came to selling Georgio's Perfume." The noise outside rattled the window again. "Why would I want to sabotage my own company? The publicity is going to ruin us."

"That's what I told Detective Briggs. He says some of the others claimed you were jealous because Autumn and Jasper seemed to be rekindling their relationship. Unfortunately, crimes of passion are very common."

Jacob grabbed a tissue and wiped his nose. "I wasn't jealous, and they weren't rekindling a relationship. That motive won't stick no matter how many ways they throw it at me."

"How can you be so sure?"

Jacob fingered the piece of toast on the plate. "I'm sure, but it's not anything I can talk about yet. I'm waiting for clarification from Baxter Redmond. He's supposed to be on his way. My dad is probably on his death bed with a stroke right now. Can't believe this has happened. I decided to go along on this trip just to get away from the office." He paused and looked down at the plate before lifting his face to me. "And to find out what town had ensnared you and charmed you into forsaking your perfumer's career for good. I stand by my Podunk comment."

"One person's Podunk is another person's paradise, and I'm not here to talk about Port Danby. How did your cologne get on the pillow that was allegedly used to smother Jasper?"

Jacob gave his head a sad shake. "No idea. I'm the only person who uses that fragrance. The chemists make me a bottle every four months. I can't remember the last time I stood in Jasper's trailer."

"And clove cigarettes? Who else smokes those?"

"No one. Including me at the moment. Yesterday morning my throat was on fire from the cold. I couldn't even think about lighting up a cigarette. But the detective found a barely used clove cigarette in my ashtray. I just couldn't remember lighting it."

"I have one other theory but don't be angry. Autumn and you are an item." I added a fleeting look of disapproval. (They really weren't right for each other.) "Is it possible that during—during any physical contact, a passionate kiss, for example that your cologne and the smell of cloves rubbed off on Autumn's clothing? There is a great deal of evidence to show she was in the trailer just before he died."

"Normally, it would have been possible. But Autumn has been staying far away from me with this cold. A runny nose doesn't make for a stunning photo shoot."

A knock sounded on the door, and Hilda popped her head inside. "Miss Pinkerton, Detective Briggs told me to let you know your time is up." She cast me a polite smile and stepped back out while I said good bye.

I stood up. "Jacob, I'm sorry that my nose sniffed out two clues that implicated you in Jasper's murder, but if it's any consolation, I truly do not think that you killed him."

He nodded at me. "Maybe you could tell that to your boyfriend with the notepad and black detective coat."

"Careful there, Mr. Georgio. I'm beginning to think you're jealous of my new life and my friends with notepads."

"Maybe a little," he said quietly and very unexpectedly.

Before I turned to leave, something he'd said struck me again.

"So you have proof that you were not jealous of Jasper and Autumn, but you can't say what that proof is until you talk to your lawyer?"

"Yes, that's right. I know it sounds strange, but hopefully, I'll be able to at least throw a plausible wrench into your detective friend's jealousy theory."

Hilda opened the door. "Briggs told me—"

"Yes, I'm sorry, Hilda. I'm leaving right now."

CHAPTER 21

$\mathscr{I}$ walked out of the interrogation room and through the hallway to the front counter. While I waited for Hilda to catch up and buzz me through, Briggs opened his office door.

"Miss Pinkerton, I need to talk to you before you leave."

I hadn't planned to stop in to see him on my way out. "I need to open the shop."

"This won't take long. I have some information about the evidence in the case."

"Already? Yes, I'd be interested to hear." Of course, I was terrified to hear at the same time, but I kept that to myself. I walked into his office, and he shut the door. His mood seemed somewhat grave, which made my stomach tighten.

He walked to his desk but rather than sit down at it, he leaned against the front of it. "The coroner has confirmed that the cause of death was suffocation, and the victim's saliva was on the pillow we found at the scene. We can conclude that it was the murder weapon. That was why the clay from the mask was on the pillow.

Nate hasn't gotten all the results back from toxicology yet so we'll know more then." He stopped and waited for my response.

"I suppose no big surprises there."

"There's more. As usual, your nose was correct. The fragrance on the pillow matched Jacob Georgio's custom cologne. The pillow also tested positive for clove cigarette. Things aren't looking great for Jacob."

"But you still don't have a motive and this murder will destroy his business."

"Jealousy can make people do crazy things," he said it almost as if he could verify that personally.

"Jacob was not jealous of Jasper. We just talked about it in—"

He put up his hand. "No, remember, that conversation was off the record. Once the lawyer arrives, Mr. Georgio can answer questions." He pushed up from his desk and walked toward me. I wasn't loving the look on his face. It assured me I wasn't going to like the next thing he said.

"Miss Pinkerton, I appreciate your help with the evidence but I'm going to have to ask you to stay clear of this investigation from this point forward."

I crossed my arms abruptly and then quickly uncrossed them to not look like an angry kid. "I can separate my personal connections from the case. I think I should have a sniff around the trailers again. Maybe I can find that cologne in another place. Autumn's clothing perhaps." Briggs stepped even closer, closer than we'd been since we nearly kissed under the mistletoe. "Lacey," he said in a deep, serious tone, "I need you to step back from this case. I gave you the coroner's information today, but from this point on, I won't be giving out any other details."

It felt as if I'd been hit in the stomach and had the breath knocked out of me. My silent, stunned response made him place his hand against the side of my arm. I stepped out of his reach.

"I understand, Detective Briggs." I made a point of lifting my chin to convince him that I was fine. Even though I clearly wasn't. "Good luck with your investigation. I might head up to the site later just to check on all my friends. If that's all right?" I asked in a snippy tone. I couldn't seem to erase just how hurt I was. "Or am I not allowed to see them?"

"Lacey, you're overreacting."

"No, I don't think I am. But thank you for informing me, Detective Briggs. Now I have a real job to attend to, not just one that I do voluntarily."

"And you've been a big help to me, Miss Pinkerton." He'd switched back to Miss Pinkerton, which only made me feel worse. "As it is, I stretch a lot of rules and ignore protocol to have you assist on the murder cases. You have to see how having you help out on a case where you know the victim and the main person of interest would be pushing the boundaries even more. And I don't think it would be wise for you emotionally. I can already see how this case has upset you."

"I'm tougher than you think," I insisted firmly, although the slight waver in my voice made a mockery of my words. "Good day, Detective Briggs." Again I lifted my chin, as I spun around and strode purposefully away. My confident departure was cut short when I met with the blasted security gate at the counter. I stood there stiffly, not turning to look at him as I waited the few awkward moments for him to buzz me through.

I walked straight to the door and out into the melee on the sidewalk. Reporters and curious onlookers all craned their necks to see who had walked out of the police station. The frenzy I'd created with my exit quieted the second they saw that it was no one of interest, just the local flower shop owner. And certainly not anyone who had anything to do with the murder case.

But then, who was to say I couldn't do a little investigative work of my own? I'd helped put Jacob in this terrible predicament, and I was going to find him a way out. I might even solve the murder before Detective Briggs. That would show him.

Newly fortified, after the terrible blow I'd received just moments before, I walked purposefully and briskly to my shop.

CHAPTER 22

The impassioned pep rally in my head, the one that had fortified my determination to solve Jasper's murder without the assistance of the local detective, had grown silent as the morning progressed. What if the clues and my investigation led me straight to the conclusion I was trying to prove wrong? What if Jacob had killed Jasper in a fit of jealous rage? All the evidence certainly pointed to it. Maybe it was better for me to just step back and let the police do their work. As hurt as I'd been by Briggs telling me in his own gentlemanly way to 'butt out' perhaps he was right. I was too close to all the people involved. My views and opinions were tainted.

Ryder was at the potting table tucking herbs into decorative window pots. I had taken advantage of the morning lull to water the plants that were sitting on the outside cart. Several women walked out of Elsie's bakery twittering excitedly about the Mr. Darcy flyer in their hands. I had tried to talk sense into my friend, but Elsie seemed to think it would work out just fine in the end. In the meantime, Lester had definitely gained an advantage in the table war with his stylish counter height tables and stools. His tables were filled, and it wasn't even a peak time of day for coffee. In fact, it was more of a peak time for lunch, and my stomach reminded me that I'd left the house without breakfast.

I finished watering the pots. The news crews had finally trickled away from the police station and the town was quiet, so quiet it was almost hard to imagine that a murder had taken place just a mile away on Maple Hill. I was surprised not to see Hazel again after her early morning visit. I hoped that she wasn't too put off by my abrupt departure. I was sure I'd see her soon. With my banishment from the case, Hazel would most likely be my only source for information about the murder.

Lola was pulling an old red toy wagon out the door to display in front of her shop. She hadn't noticed me standing amongst my plant carts. I called her name, but she didn't hear me.

I carried the watering pot inside the store and put it in the sink. "Ryder, I'm going to walk across the street and see if Lola wants to get some lunch. I'm starved. Does that work for you?"

"Yep, my mom made me biscuits and gravy this morning with a side of sausage. I won't need lunch for awhile."

"Hmm, biscuits and gravy. My mom used to make those on cold Saturday mornings. Sometimes I just want to crawl back into my childhood and back into one of those Saturday mornings where the only things I had to worry about were which cartoon to watch and which friend to invite for a sleepover."

"Those were the days, huh? You go ahead, boss. And they might not be the same as your mom's but don't forget that Franki makes a rockin' plate of biscuits and gravy."

I pointed at him. "See, I need to think out of the box like you. I was thinking sandwich because it's lunch, but last I heard there was no law against breakfast at lunch. I'm going for it. Can I bring you back anything?"

"Nope, I'm good."

I grabbed my coat and headed across the street. Lola had gone back into the antique shop. Her dog, Late Bloomer, met me at the door. I stopped to give him a good rub before heading around the maze of shelves and displays to the counter. Lola was nowhere in sight.

"Hey there, I'm in the mood for Franki's biscuits and gravy." My words ricocheted off the displays, but no answer bounced back with them. "Lola," I called again.

Lola emerged from the office. She had a few old pictures clutched in her fingers. With all that had happened, I'd forgotten about the strange picture with the ghostly figure.

"Do you want to get some lunch?"

Lola walked past me and placed the pictures on the counter. She still hadn't said a word, highly unusual for loquacious Lola.

"I mean it doesn't have to be biscuits and gravy. You can order whatever you like," I added, confused by her silence.

She looked up at me with a sort of 'oh I didn't see you there' expression.

"Lola, hello? Have you heard anything I said?"

Lola pushed her curly red hair back behind her ear. "Yes, sorry. Lunch sounds good. I was still thinking about these pictures." She spread out four pictures on the counter. I was almost hesitant to look at them. They certainly had Lola in a fog.

I cautiously approached the counter as if someone might jump out of the pictures at me. Lola spun one around for me to look at. It was the same Georgian house, a large sprawling brick building with white columns and a half round portico over the front door. A woman, the same woman from the first picture, was dressed in full petticoats playing a game of croquet on the front lawn. There were several children playing the game along with the woman. It seemed a wholesome and pleasant enough scene. I looked up at Lola, who had been silently waiting for my reaction. "They are playing croquet," I said lamely.

Lola huffed brusquely, lifting several curly red strands of hair from her forehead. Her finger tapped the picture. "Look closely at the front stoop."

Rather than lift the picture, I lowered my face over the image and my gaze landed on the shady spot beneath the portico. I sucked in a sharp breath. The milky haze from the earlier picture was pressed against one of the white columns and once again the image of a tall, rather dapper looking man dressed in early nineteenth century Regency fashion seemed to be standing in the mist, his piercing dark eyes riveted on the woman playing croquet.

"That's just not possible," I uttered once I caught my breath.

Lola spun the first picture around. "And yet we are both seeing it. And since he's standing in this photo too, the first one can't just be a problem with the film or development process."

"I guess not but there's still no explanation. Maybe this man just has a really rich aura and we're seeing it around him in the pictures," I suggested and was met immediately with a turned lip and raised brow. "Yes, I suppose that sounds just as far-fetched as the alternative."

"Which is?" Lola asked.

"That the man is a ghost."

She released a breath. "Good. I was waiting for you to say it because frankly I've been starting to question my sanity over these pictures."

I picked up the first picture and turned it around. Someone had written the name Mary Richards, Firefly Junction, 1859 on the back. "There's some information on the back."

"I know. Instead of spending the last two hours dusting antiques I've been doing a little research. Firefly Junction is a small town on the eastern base of the Blue Ridge Mountains. It was a small mining town through most of the century but when the coal was drained out of the area, most families moved on. In the 1920's, it was revived by moonshiners and they made some good money with their stills. They used it to restore some of the town." She waved that information off as inconsequential. "It wasn't until I found an article about Cider Ridge Inn that things got interesting."

"Cider Ridge Inn?"

She pointed at the brick house in the picture. "There was a few articles about it with pictures because of its unusual past. It was built in 1815 by Cleveland Ross, a wealthy businessman who wanted a charming escape for his young bride, Bonnie. She loved the Blue Ridge Mountains, so he bought a parcel of land and had the house built for her. A few years into the marriage, Cleveland heard word from his family in England that a distant cousin, Edward Beckett, had gotten into some legal trouble. Apparently he was quite the rogue and black sheep but he was also a member of the gentry. The family decided to ship him off to America to save the family any further embarrassment. Gambling and women, I deduced from the few scant pieces of information I could find."

"I think I know where this is going. Edward Beckett had an affair with Cleveland's young wife."

"Yes. Which led to a duel. Naturally."

"Naturally."

"Beckett was shot in the shoulder. He didn't die right away. It seems that a very distraught Bonnie had the servants carry him inside the house where she nursed him and watched over him until he died. Cleveland sent his wife to live out the rest of her days with relatives and sold the house to the Richards family."

I looked down at the pictures and the ghostly image standing on the porch. "Do you think we're looking at Edward's ghost?"

"It would explain what we're seeing and why his clothes are so outdated. The Herbert family bought the place in 1920, presumably with moonshine money, after it had sat vacant for decades. They turned it into Cider Ridge Inn."

"You have done some very good detective work, my friend. And what a story. I wonder who is living there now?"

"It's in a family trust but it's vacant. Too many unexplained disturbances."

"I'll bet. These pictures?"

Lola shook her head. "Not sure how they got into the box of relics. My parents are on the east coast so they must have discovered them with the rest of the attic finds." She swept the photos into her hand and put them aside. "Enough of that. These stupid things are taking up too much of my time. I'm way behind on my work. Let's go to lunch. Unraveling ghost stories has made me hungry."

CHAPTER 23

*H*azel looked as if she was bursting with news as she waited for me to finish with a customer. She impatiently tapped her feet on the tile floor as she pretended to look at the bouquet examples in the window. I hoped that she had some good news. Although it was probably silly to expect any good news after someone had been murdered.

I finished the order for a silver wedding anniversary to take place in March. It was a big order of purple irises and white roses for a party of a hundred people. I was thankful the party was still a month away, giving Ryder and me plenty of time to design arrangements and order supplies. The woman paid her deposit and left, pleased with the flowers she'd picked.

Hazel nearly jumped out of her coat to start talking the second the door shut. "The press finally got bored and left, but I think this town's haunted house attraction is going to get a lot of publicity. When they couldn't find out anything newsworthy about the current murder, they started taking pictures of the manor and delving into its sordid history. A murder-suicide of an entire prominent family made for an interesting diversion for the reporters. I was just glad to see the last news van roll away. This awfulness is not going to bode well for Georgio's Perfume."

I placed the silver wedding anniversary order into the binder and joined Hazel on the stool side of the counter. "Have you heard anything new?" I asked. "Did Baxter Redmond get to town?"

"I believe he arrived. Aside from what we've been telling each other, the rest of us are mostly in the dark." She unzipped her coat. "You probably know more than we do since you're assisting the detective."

"No, I'm not, actually. It's true he asks me to help with evidence collection from time to time, but I'm sitting this one out. Involuntarily," I added.

"Oh, why is that? I thought you and your nose had helped him solve more than one important case. I remember reading about some famous food blogger with a rabid fan base who got killed in the same hotel where we're staying this week." Hazel pushed off her coat. It seemed she'd be staying for awhile. Ryder had gone on a late lunch break, and I was actually pleased to have some company. It was one of those days where I was better off not left to my own thoughts.

"Yes, I did help Detective Briggs with that case. But this one is too close to home. At least according to the detective."

"That's a shame. Then again, maybe he's right." She had accepted the reasoning much easier than me. She sat on the stool and absently played with a few of the stray pieces of ribbon on the island. "I did find out a few juicy nuggets that you might not have heard now that the nice—and handsome—detective has cut you off."

I crinkled my nose at her phrase choice.

"You're right. My bad. Not cut you off but turned off the flow of information," she corrected. She shifted her bottom to get a more solid purchase on the stool as if whatever she had to tell me might just blow her right off the seat. "Remember I told you that Autumn and Jasper had planned to do some spa treatments while waiting for the rain to stop?"

"And according to the evidence in the trailer that was true."

"I know." She squished her face like a kid tasting broccoli. "Poor Jasper died with pink clay mask all over his face."

"How did you know?"

"Alexander told me. He's the one who found Jasper."

"Oh, of course."

"Anyhow, that brings me back to Alexander. Autumn told Lydia and me and, I can only assume, the police that she saw Alexander storming angrily out of Jasper's trailer just as she was walking over with her facial supplies. She asked him what was wrong, but he barely grunted a word in response. He just kept marching, fists curled, and nostrils flaring."

"Wow, that's a big reaction for Alexander. He's pretty mild mannered. Maybe Autumn was exaggerating."

"That could be. She's been known to do that. I even considered that she was making it up just to put another suspect into the detective's headlights," Hazel suggested. "After all, she and Jacob are an item," she added unnecessarily. "And then, of course, there was the discovery of a striped sock beneath Jasper's couch that didn't belong to him. Autumn was freaking out because the detective showed it to her and asked if it was hers. Which it was."

"Perfectly logical line of questioning." I walked over and picked up the broom from the work area and began sweeping the day's trimmings into a pile. It had been a long day, and I was looking forward to going home to be nudged and kneaded by my cat and glowered at by my crow for leaving him in his cage for the day. "Why was her sock there? I assumed it had something to do with spa day."

"Supposedly Autumn was planning on putting the mask on her feet too, but Jasper said he was tired and wanted to nap. That's when spa day ended, apparently. Autumn was mad. She searched for the sock but couldn't find it so she just put on her shoes, swept up her things and left. At least that's what Autumn told me that she told the police."

I looked up from my task. "Do you have any reason not to believe her?"

Hazel shrugged. "Autumn is not exactly a pillar of honesty. She obviously left upset with Jasper." Hazel had never cared for Autumn and it seemed she'd managed to talk herself into the possibility that the model was a suspect. "According to the time-line, Autumn was the last person to see Jasper alive."

"Other than the murderer," I added. "Hazel, early cancellation on an impromptu spa day is hardly enough to drive someone to murder."

She sloughed off the suspicious tone in her voice. "You're right. I'm just trying to make some sense of it all. I'm just so distraught about poor Jacob. Unless, of course, he's guilty, then I'm disappointed with myself for not really knowing the man. I have, after all, been his assistant for many years."

"And a good, loyal one at that. That's why you're searching for ways to prove him innocent. I feel the same sense of loyalty to Jacob, and he doesn't even deserve it from me. I just can't believe he'd do anything so heinous."

"Me neither. Now that you're not helping with the investigation, I guess we both just have to wait and see how this plays out."

My shoulders slumped. I hated being out in the cold on any case, and most especially on this one. "You know, Hazel, with you sort of still on the inside of this, maybe we can work together and find puzzle pieces."

She brightened. "Like private investigators?"

"Yes, like that."

She hopped off the stool and saluted me. "At your service, PI Pinkerton. If I find out anything I will report it directly to you. And if you hear anything, you can report it to me."

"Sounds like a plan, Hazel. Who needs that nice and, admittedly handsome, Detective Briggs? We'll figure this out on our own."

CHAPTER 24

*M*y plans for a quiet evening with my pets were dashed just before closing when a glum looking Elsie walked into the shop.

"You were right, Pink. I'm a silly goose."

I pulled on my coat and reached for my scarf. "Is this about Mr. Darcy?"

"Yes. I'm trying to decide if I overestimated or underestimated people. I was sure everyone would reason out that they wouldn't be having tea with the real Mr. Darcy. But this morning, Ingrid Baines from over on Culpepper Road came into the bakery excited as a schoolgirl who'd been asked to the prom. She told me that her sister Betsy was flying in from California to meet Colin Firth. That was when it finally struck me that I'd made a big mistake."

"Oh, Elsie, did you tell her the truth?"

At sixty, Elsie was one of the fittest people on the planet. She had a posture that was so perfect, the word slouch wasn't even in her vocabulary. Or at least it wasn't until that moment. Her shoulders crumpled forward. "I couldn't. I didn't have the heart to tell her the truth. She looked so excited." Her face lit up with an idea. "Do you think I might be able to talk him into coming to Port Danby?"

"Who?"

"Mr. Darcy. Colin Firth. Maybe if I promised him a lifetime supply of my baked goods."

I tilted my head. "Pretty sure that idea isn't going to work. I'm sure he's a gentleman and a nice man, but I believe he's an Oscar winning actor. He might not have a lot of time to drop by Port Danby for tea and cupcakes."

Her shoulders deflated again. "You're right. I'm just getting sillier. Boy, I've learned my lesson. I no longer care how many people are sitting at my tables." She waved her arm in the direction of her brother's coffee shop. "Everyone can sit at Lester's fancy tables. Makes no difference to me." Since she'd made the same declaration many times, I just smiled and nodded.

"Elsie, there's still time for you to put out a retraction or clarification flyer. That way everyone will expect Mr. Darcy to be cardboard."

"Do you think?"

"Yes."

"I'm going to lose so much business over this, Pink. I should have listened to you in the first place. Hey, I'm skipping my run tonight. I was going to head over to Franki's for her chili and corn bread. I need comfort food, not icy wind and sore calves. Would you join me? I don't feel like eating alone tonight."

"Uh, sure. I never turn down Franki's chili."

I finished draping myself in my winter gear, and Elsie and I headed down the sidewalk to Franki's. I hadn't planned to eat at the diner twice in one day, but it seemed Elsie really needed the company. Her husband, Hank, spent more than half the year traveling for business, so Elsie was left alone a lot. She never seemed to mind it and swore those months of independence were what made her marriage to Hank so strong. But tonight she was feeling down, and I knew she needed some supportive companionship.

"What is happening with the murder case?" Elsie asked as we walked through the diner parking lot. "I saw a flurry of activity in front of the police station earlier today. I guess the victim was well known?"

"Jasper was the face of Georgio's Perfume. You've no doubt seen many pictures of him in magazines and on billboards." My phone buzzed as I opened the door for Elsie.

"I'm sure I have." Elsie walked past and into the diner.

I glanced at my phone. It was a text from Ryder. "Sent you a rainbow picture. You never got a chance to see them." The picture was still downloading, so I stuck my phone back into my pocket.

Franki was already off for the evening, which was a shame. Franki Rumple, the owner of Franki's Diner, was always a good source of information. Her diner was a popular stop for both locals and visitors. It was just a cute, casual diner, but the quality of her food made her place extremely popular. Much like Elsie, Franki was a true dynamo with boundless energy and talent. And when she wasn't running her extremely successful restaurant, she was busy at home with her four teenagers.

Elsie and I found a table near the door and scooted into the seats. Franki's son, Taylor, walked over to take our order. I knew it was Taylor only because of his nametag. His twin brother, Tyler, was an exact duplicate. They were impossible to tell apart.

"Your mom mentioned that you boys had started working at the diner in the evenings," I said.

Taylor smiled proudly. "Figured it was time to start helping Mom out. Let me guess. Chili and corn bread?"

Elsie held up two fingers.

"Two bowls of chili coming up." He tucked away his order pad and left.

I watched him hurry to the kitchen to turn in the order. "I

guess the boys are starting to mature. I'm glad. Franki's got a lot on her plate as a single mom."

"True," Elsie agreed. "I wish I could find good, reliable help for the bakery."

I held back a smile. "Maybe you need to lower your standards a bit."

"Said the flower shop owner who landed the most marvelous shop assistant in the world." Elsie tucked a gray strand of hair back into the clips that held the rest of her toffee and gray hair in a neat, efficient bun.

"You're right. I should just seal my lips on this topic. I don't want to jinx myself."

Elsie slumped back against the vinyl seat. It was her third slump of the evening. It was usually Elsie giving the advice, but tonight, it seemed, she needed to be on the receiving end for a change.

"Don't worry, Elsie. Everyone within a fifty mile radius is addicted to your baked goods. People might be slightly upset about the Mr. Darcy promise, but you won't lose business. Maybe you could give every Valentine's Day visitor one of those delicious caramel kisses as a gift. They'll get lost in the brown sugar goodness and all will be forgiven."

"That's a good idea. I hope you're right. One thing is for sure, next time you try and warn me about one of my cockamamie plans, I'm going to listen."

The front door opened, and Lydia walked in with Alexander. She caught a glimpse of me as she stood at the take-out counter. She waved weakly. Alexander looked like a shell of his former self, drawn and pale with dark rings under his eyes. My mind shot back to the morning when Hazel had shown up at my house unexpectedly. She had offered her theory that Lydia might have been behind the murder. According to Hazel, she had motive. Lydia had recently discovered that Jasper and Autumn made three times the amount of money she did for a photo shoot. That would be a slap in the face for any faithful employee. But was it enough to drive her to murder? I didn't know Lydia well. We'd never really connected on a friendship level, but I always thought highly of her and her talent. Still, it wouldn't hurt to have a quick chat, just to get a sense of how she was feeling. From where I sat, one thing was obvious. Alexander was far more distressed than Lydia.

"Elsie, if you'll excuse me a moment, a few of my old acquaintances are here. I just want to see how they're doing."

"Sure."

I slipped out of the seat and headed to the take-out counter. There was a brief, quiet hug session.

"How is everything?" I asked.

Alexander couldn't work up a response. The hug had caused tears to well up in his eyes. Lydia, on the other hand, had no problem speaking up.

"Of course the last thing we needed was to be swarmed with news crews this morning. We're all trying to come to grips with it, and we were having to duck around to avoid cameras and reporters."

"Yes, at least it seems they've gone for now," I noted and cast a weak smile toward Alexander. He was still speechless.

"I hope that detective gets to the bottom of this soon. It's terrible publicity for the company," Lydia continued. It was obvious her rather callous disregard for the tragedy itself was upsetting Alexander even more. I decided to put a quick end to the conversation.

"I'm sure everything will be sorted out soon. Have you spoken to Jacob?" I tossed in a quick attempt to find out just what was going on with the investigation.

Lydia shrugged. "If only they'd tell us something. Jacob hasn't spoken to any of us. He's with that arrogant old lawyer Redmond. We've heard nothing."

Their food came.

"Let me know if there's anything I can do, and tell everyone I'm thinking about them."

"Thanks, Lacey, we will."

Alexander nodded at me as they turned to leave. I pulled my phone out of my pocket on the way back to the table. The rainbow picture had arrived.

I sat down at the table. Elsie was buttering her corn bread. "Those were people you worked with?"

"Not directly, but yes. They worked for the same company." I rubbed my thumb over the picture to open it. "Sorry, Ryder sent me a picture, and I don't want to hurt his feelings by not commenting on it."

Ryder had been bragging that the camera on his new phone took great pictures. He was right. The arch of a rainbow hung like a crystal light prism over Pickford Beach. The colors sparkled in an otherwise gloomy, gray sky.

"Look how pretty this rainbow is." I turned the phone to Elsie. She pulled out her reading glasses and put them on. Even with glasses, she squinted at the picture. It seemed odd considering the rainbow was hard to miss, glasses or not. She covered her mouth to stifle a laugh. "Now that's a fun coincidence. Or is it irony? I get those mixed up."

"I don't think a rainbow is a coincidence or irony. I think it's physics. Not sure what you mean."

Elsie pointed at the screen. "It's just that there are two men holding hands on the beach beneath the rainbow. Like the symbol."

I spun the phone back around. I'd been so focused on the rainbow, I hadn't noticed the people on the beach, also focused on the rainbow. And Elsie was right. There were two men holding hands gazing at the colors in the sky. And they were two men I knew. Suddenly it was clear why Jacob said he had proof he wasn't jealous of Jasper and Autumn. The picture would also explain why

Alexander looked as if he'd just lost someone very dear to him. He had.

I stretched up to look out the window. The diner was across the street from the police station. Detective Briggs' car was still parked out front. "Elsie, if you don't mind, I'm going to eat fast. I need to go see Detective Briggs before he leaves for the night. You and your little ironic coincidence just put a new twist in the murder case."

CHAPTER 25

$\mathcal{I}$ reached the station, but the door was locked. I peered through the tinted glass and between the broken slats on the blinds. Hilda and Officer Chinmoor's desks were dark. The only light was coming from Briggs' office.

I pulled out my phone. I sent a text to Ryder letting him know the picture was beautiful and asking him what time he took it. He wrote back that it was Wednesday morning at seven.

I sent the picture to Briggs with no text. I decided to see if he noticed anything significant in the picture. I certainly hadn't until Elsie pointed it out.

I paced in front of the station to keep warm and waited for a return text. It took longer than I'd hoped, and with each passing minute, I felt more and more deflated. Briggs really didn't want anything to do with me anymore. As that depressing thought took hold, a text came through.

"Very nice rainbow."

I texted back. "It is. Do you see anything of note in the picture?"

A significant pause followed. "Yes. I see. Interesting. When was this taken?"

"Wednesday at seven in the morning. Ryder shot it on Pickford Beach."

"Did you know that Jasper was seeing Alexander?"

"Not until—" I stopped texting. My fingers were too cold, and I kept hitting the wrong keys. I decided to call him.

"Hello."

"Hello. My fingers were too cold to keep texting."

"Why? Where are you?"

"Outside the police station."

Seconds later another light went on and Briggs unlocked the front door. I stepped inside and turned to watch him lock up the door. He spun around and our gazes locked for a long moment. We said nothing for that stretch of time, but it felt like words were spoken.

"I was hoping you'd still be talking to me. I'm sorry I had to take you off the case."

I held up my hand. "I understand. Of course, there's no law that says I can't do a little mystery solving on my own. And I think this picture is a big clue."

"How is that?"

"Motive. Jacob wasn't jealous of Jasper and Autumn. Surely that's obvious now."

"If he knew about Jasper's relationship with Alexander, why didn't he say something?"

I was stopped by his question as I searched for a reasonable answer. "I'm not sure, but when I spoke to Jacob he said he had information that would shut down the jealousy motive. He must have known."

"Did anyone else know? I'm going to assume you were unaware of it."

"I had no idea. And I have to say, Hazel, the woman who I

thought knew everything about everyone didn't seem to know either. Otherwise, she would have mentioned it. It's all kind of strange."

He gave me that sort of empathetic expression, almost a 'good try, kiddo' look. I would have been irritated if he hadn't looked so handsome doing it. "Lacey"—there came the sympathetic tone to go with the empathetic look on his face—"You know this doesn't mean much. There are always other possible motives."

"Yes, which brings me to someone else who was on site and who was close to Jasper. According to my friend, Hazel, who knows everything that goes on at the company." I lifted the phone to point out the picture. "Except the relationship between Jasper and Alexander," I added quickly. "Hazel told me that Lydia found out that the models, Autumn and Jasper, made three times as much as her, and she was plenty angry about it. Who wouldn't be? She does the bulk of the work. They just stand around looking spectacular. Or stood, I guess. At least for one of them." My voice trailed off. Suddenly my attempt to throw a few more people of interest into the mix seemed foolish.

"Look, I know this whole thing isn't easy on you. It's one of the reasons I took you off the case. You have to be able to look at an investigation objectively and knowing everyone involved makes that impossible. I'll go talk to Alexander and Lydia again. It seems they both left off some important details about their relationships with Jasper. Lydia had nothing but gushing praise for him. At the time, I thought it sounded a little forced. Alexander mentioned that he'd take care of notifying Jasper's family and making funeral arrangements, which seemed above his duty as a friend. But the photo obviously adds another layer to his relationship with the deceased."

"And ask Alexander why he was so angry when he left Jasper's trailer."

"That already came up when I talked to Alexander. He said it was just a friend's quarrel. I guess it was more than that given this new revelation."

I decided to try one more strategy to get back into helping him with the case. "I understand the whole objectivity concept, but doesn't it sometimes help to be a little subjective or at least have someone on your side who everyone feels comfortable talking to? I was in the diner just now talking to both Lydia and Alexander, and I can tell you that Lydia was almost more upset about the reporters harassing them than losing a close colleague. Alexander looked just as one might expect after losing a loved one."

"So you want to be a double agent and talk to your friends with a kind face and then turn around and tell me what they've said and how they reacted?"

His question took the wind right out of my sails. "No, not when you phrase it like that. I guess it would be sort of traitorous of me. Just like sniffing out all kinds of evidence that pointed to Jacob." I sighed and pushed my phone back into my pocket. "This is such an awful position to be in. And to think I was enjoying myself as assistant sleuth to the Port Danby Police. Can you at least tell me where you're at with Jacob? Did his lawyer come?"

He pondered my request for a moment. "Jacob is at the hotel with his lawyer."

"Baxter Redmond is a brusque, fast talking man. But he might be a poor choice for this predicament. I think he is more of a corporate lawyer."

"Yes, I got that impression. Jacob answered all the questions. He is sticking to his alibi. He spent the morning sick in bed. He has no explanation for the cologne or clove cigarette odor on the pillow. And we couldn't find any significant traces on Autumn's clothing." He looked slightly uncomfortable about the last revelation.

"It's all right, Detective Briggs. I had the same idea myself. Jacob told me Autumn had been staying clear of his germs."

The slight grin on his face had a touch of pride. "You are

certainly thinking more and more like a detective." Briggs looked weary as he combed his hair back with his fingers. "It's late. I need to finish some paperwork and you should get home." He walked me to the door.

"I could go with you when you interview Lydia and Alexander. You know, if you needed me." I looked at him with big, hopeful eyes.

Briggs shook his head and unlocked the door. "Good night, Miss Pinkerton."

I stepped out into the icy night air and turned back to him. "Good night, Detective Briggs."

CHAPTER 26

*N*evermore met me at the front door. I temporarily considered that he was just excited to see me, but it seemed he was more excited to see what the pesky squirrel was doing in Dash's mulberry tree. The cat shot past me without so much as a whisker twitch or tail flick. He raced across the yard and up the trunk of the mulberry, disappearing quickly into its branches.

Kingston, however, did have a greeting for me. It was more of an angry screech than a hello, but it was still a step above the cat's greeting. I closed the front door and opened Kingston's cage. I decided to leave my winter gear on. Something told me it was going to take some clever cat owner tricks to get Nevermore down from the tree. Cat luring had not been on my list of activities for the night. I was tired and slightly grumpy from the day.

I had to admit it was nice talking to Detective Briggs, even if I couldn't get him to budge on my participation in the investigation. That part had been disappointing. But what he'd said also made perfect sense. (Something the man was irritatingly good at.) I was already devastated having to point out that the cologne and cloves on the pillow belonged to Jacob. I didn't need to add salt to that wound by implicating other people. Or worse, finding more evidence that pointed to Jacob. At the moment, it seemed the only thing Briggs really had on Jacob was the cologne and clove cigarette. It seemed like a flimsy case. I knew Briggs well enough to know that he thought so too. It seemed he was going to have to find something more significant to charge Jacob. Of course, that was just my assessment. Or at least my hopeful assessment.

I grabbed the hardboiled eggs I'd cooked for Kingston and crumbled them into the dish on his perch. I glanced out the front window to Nevermore's favorite place on the porch. It seemed he was still in the tree. I decided I didn't need a squirrel's untimely death on my conscience, so I walked back out armed with a bag of Never's favorite treats

The light was on in Dash's garage, and his truck was in the driveway. He was always building, cutting, hammering or sanding something out in his garage. The house he'd bought next door to me came with a pleasant price tag because it needed a major dose of TLC. And Dash was definitely giving it plenty. When he wasn't out working on boats in the marina, Dash was working on his house. And, apparently, flying the deep blue skies whenever he had access to a plane.

I trudged across the winter brown grass in Dash's front yard and stopped beneath the massive mulberry growing in the center of his lawn. The tree's gigantic roots caused the lawn to crest and curve, but I found a secure place to stand beneath the maze of branches. A few green buds were showing the signs of an early spring. Otherwise, the tree was devoid of all its lush foliage. The sky above was a dark slate gray, the color of Nevermore's fur, and the stars were only starting to turn on their lights. Fortunately, my cat had grown just fat and clumsy enough from his endless hours on the couch to make him easy to find. A cluster of thin branches high up in the dome of the tree shook frenetically. Something told me the squirrel had slipped down and away from his chubby predator long ago. Leaving my cat, disappointed and alone, high up in the mulberry.

Nevermore was a good ten feet up, and my tree climbing days were behind me. I held up the foil bag of treats and rattled it. Normally, I could shake the treat bag from anywhere in the house, and Nevermore would be instantly at my side, twirling around my ankles. But not this time. His big amber eyes stared longingly at the bag, and he let out a low, mournful meow. He took a small step forward with his front paw but froze when his entire body wriggled precariously on the fragile perch.

I hadn't heard Dashwood walk up behind me until he was standing next to me. He was wearing a dark blue flannel shirt, my favorite because it contrasted nicely with his dark blond hair. He stared up into the tree and scratched his chin as he seemed to be assessing the situation.

I stared up with him. "The moment you realize your cat is more couch potato than cat." I held up the treats. "I guess that makes me an enabler with all the goodies I toss his way. And that reality's hitting me extra hard as I stare up at my gray striped pillow from this angle."

Dash repositioned himself under a thick branch that seemed to be the hub for the myriad of branches Nevermore was standing on. "I could give it a shake. Is it really true that cats always land on their feet?"

"Possibly, but I think that theory is only true when the cat is lithe, supple and not carrying a large belly of fat."

Dash looked up at Nevermore. "Those paws do look a little frail for a comfortable landing. And he looks as if he's accepted his fate that he's never going to leave the tree again. There's no way to get a ladder up into all these branches." Without another word, Dash turned to the gnarled trunk of the tree. He grabbed a few

135

sturdy lower branches and hoisted himself effortlessly into the tree.

"Don't fall," I said quickly.

"That's my goal," he answered as he lifted his foot to a higher branch and pushed through the thinner branches and debris. "I knew I should have had this tree trimmed last month."

He stepped with one foot onto a long, outstretched branch that, along with his six foot height would get him close enough to my silly cat. He pushed down on the branch several times, checking to see if it would hold his weight. There was nothing to indicate it wouldn't, no ominous cracking sound or major shift in position.

Dash reached up to hold some branches above for extra support as he slid his feet sideways along the branch. He had incredible balance. Not to mention he played the hero part extremely well. And he looked exceptionally handsome doing it.

Nevermore watched the entire scene below with feline indifference until Dash got close enough to reach up and grab the cat. His big hand was just about to wrap around Nevermore's rotund body when my ridiculous tabby shot off his perch and came down the maze of branches like a ball bouncing back and forth through a pinball machine. Nevermore hit the ground and ran toward the front porch.

The branch beneath Dash's feet proved to be fickle after all. A crackling sound grew louder. It started to give way. My hand flew to my mouth as Dash jumped over to a more secure spot near the trunk and then down to the ground. He glanced down quickly at his hand and then tried, unsuccessfully, to hide it behind him.

"Did that ungrateful bum scratch you on the way down?"

Dash shook his head. "It's nothing."

"Nonsense. I have special antibacterial scrub for cat scratches because my cat is a knucklehead about having his claws out at the wrong time. I think it stems from latent mommy issues or something. They weaned him way too young." I motioned toward my house. "Follow me and I'll fix you up. It's the least I can do after you risked life and limb." I pointed to the tree. "*And* limb for my cat." I looked back at him as he followed me to the porch. "Thank you, by the way. I think you went way beyond your job description as a helpful neighbor tonight."

Nevermore shot inside the second I opened the door. (Not out of shame but because he'd been away from his food dish for longer than usual.)

"Hey, Kingston." Dash walked over to say hello to the crow while I walked into my bathroom for the first aid kit.

I returned to the living room. Dash was hand feeding Kingston a sunflower seed. My neighbor looked exceptionally tall and broad shouldered in my small front room.

"You are brave. My cat leaves you bleeding in a tree, and yet, you are fearlessly holding out a tiny seed to my bird's long black beak."

"Guess those last few seconds in the tree made me feel immortal." Kingston took the seed from his fingers.

"Come out here to the living room and have a seat near the light. I promise to be gentle."

"That's a shame," he retorted with sly smile. There was no denying that Dash and I'd had more than our share of moments of heavy duty flirting. But it had never gone further than that. And I never expected it to go past smiling and playful jokes. I wasn't sure how I'd concluded that. Dash was, technically, the most sought after man in town. Kate Yardley, the gorgeous, stylish and somewhat snooty owner of the Mod Frock Boutique practically fell out onto the sidewalk on her tall, vintage boots every time Dash strolled through town. Even Elsie's head turned when he walked past. And I'd snuck my share of peeks at my neighbor too. But there had always been something in the back of my mind telling me to steer clear of anything more serious with the man. Something told me he would only lead to unnecessary complications in my otherwise smooth sailing life. At least it was smooth sailing until the Georgio's Perfume crew rolled into town.

Dash had only twice been inside my house for a brief visit. He looked around at my simple decor. Being a flower shop owner I always had at least two vases of flowers, one for the small table in the front window and one for the end table near the sofa. I'd brought home a cluster of pale pink peonies and a bunch of purple lilac that were too past their prime to sell.

"I guess you can't ever be wooed by a nice bouquet of flowers." Dash relaxed back and held out his hand. Nevermore had left three parallel, inch long scratches just above his knuckles.

"I could still be wooed, but the bouquet would have to contain some spectacular, rare species, so rare that I can't even name them for you now. However, when it comes to chocolate, I'm easily wooed. Doesn't have to be rare or spectacular. I'm pretty easy when it comes to chocolate."

"I will have to keep that in mind." I wasn't sure if it was because I was almost holding his hand as I tended to the scratches or if he was just in an extra playful mood, but Dash was giving off some very flirty vibes. I wasn't hating it either. I wondered if I'd formed an opinion of him too early.

He grew noticeably quiet as I rubbed the antibacterial over the cuts.

"I'm not hurting you, am I?"

He laughed quietly. "Not at all. The opposite in fact. You have a nice touch."

I released his fingers.

"Sorry, that was too forward," he said.

"Not at all. I was just done cleaning the scratches. Would you like a bandage?" I held up one of my decorative ones. "I have some with little daisies on them."

"No, I think I'll survive. Bandages don't really stick around in my line of work. I thank you for your first aid." He stood up, once again filling my small front room with his impressive build. "I'd still love to take you on that plane ride if you have time. Saturday? I've been keeping track of the weather. It's going to be nice."

I walked him to the door. "I've got to say that invitation sounds just a little too fun to resist."

"Terrific." He stopped before walking out. "It won't be a long trip. I'll have you back in Port Danby before you get your land legs back." He had an infectious smile.

I smiled back at him. "Sounds amazing."

"Great. Dress warm. See you Saturday." He headed down the porch.

I leaned my face out into the cold night air. "Thanks again for saving my cat."

"I think he saved himself," he called back. He waved and lumbered on his long legs to his own yard.

CHAPTER 27

brisk breeze had kicked up bringing a hard chill for the night. I tucked myself into bed with a book, but the day's events, and for that matter, the evening's events, both at the police station and at home, had given me too much to think about. After reading the same line four times, I decided to close the book and try to work myself into a fretful night's sleep.

My phone chimed and vibrated on my nightstand. My mom was one of the few people I knew who preferred phone conversations to texts. She insisted it was because she wouldn't know if she was actually talking to me or to 'the lunatic kidnapper who'd wrested the phone from me as he grabbed me kicking and screaming to his car'. She said she had to hear my voice or she would be worried sick. I'd suggested a few security questions, those only a mom could answer. Like the day I bought my first bra, (last day of summer before seventh grade and it was more for self esteem than *support*), the name of my first crush (Steven Foxworth, the obligatory best friend's big brother crush) or the one food I hated to get in my lunch bag but that she always packed (a hardboiled egg because of the embarrassing odor that followed a cooked egg). But she insisted she had to intermittently hear my voice or lose sleep.

"Hey, Mom, it's later than usual. Everything all right?"

I could hear the television blasting in the next room where Dad had most likely fallen asleep watching sports.

"I should say not," she huffed. "And to think you nearly married a cold-blooded murderer. I knew Jacob was no good. It was a lucky day when your wedding was called off."

I pulled the phone away for a second to stifle the sound, then returned it to my ear. Mom was still ranting on about how she'd never trusted Jacob Georgio and that rich people were always bad.

"Mom. Mom. Mom." I used my calm voice three times, but she continued to talk over me. I switched to something altogether more shrill. "Mom!"

"What!" she shrilled back.

"You need to slow down. First, remember that you were extremely despondent when I broke up with Jacob. I believe the words 'making the worst mistake of your life' were being bandied about for a few weeks."

"Not true. Right from the start I told you he wasn't trustworthy."

"See, this is why I wish you would text, Mom. Then I'd have proof. Anyhow, that doesn't matter. I don't know what they're saying in the newspapers, but Jacob hasn't been charged with murder yet."

"Yet. That word just says it all. So you think he will be? Oh, wait until I tell your dad. He thought I was jumping the gun on declaring him a murderer."

"Yeah, you are. You're jumping a big gun, a canon-sized gun. So stop."

"And did you have any part in the investigation with that handsome Detective Briggs? It seems you have a bit of a thing for the detective."

"Jumping yet another gun, Mom. I don't even know where you're coming up with this stuff."

"You said as much when you and Aunt Sheila were playing cards and sipping those rum drinks." A beeping sound echoed in the background. "I've got to get tomorrow morning's muffins out of the oven. I'm putting you on speaker phone."

"Wait. No." It was too late. She spent the next minute trying to figure out how to put the phone on speaker. In the meantime, the oven was beeping like a backward driving garbage truck. During the interim, I chastised myself for drinking too much rum. It always made me loose lipped. I quickly tried to remember just what I'd said to Aunt Sheila that made my mom think there was something going on between Detective Briggs and me. I drew a blank. Those darn rum drinks.

Mom came back to the phone. "I gave up on the speaker phone and just pulled the muffins out of the oven. Now, where were we? Oh yes, I was about to recite that wise old saying reminding you that 'you think you know someone until you realize you don't'."

"I don't think there's any such saying, and if there is, I'm sure it's not quite so convoluted. And I know Jacob. I broke up with him because of it. But I don't think he's capable of murder, and you shouldn't either until we know for certain. Here's my wise old saying, 'innocent until proven guilty'."

"Hmm, best banana nut muffins I've ever made," Mom mumbled over a mouthful.

"I thought those were for morning."

"Yes, they are. But they are so delicious fresh out of the oven. You never answered my question about working with that nice detective. Is he single?"

I laughed. Even when she was in full mom mode, it was hard not to laugh.

"What? Perfectly logical question," she insisted.

"Yes, I suppose. For a mom. I just love the way you jump from topic to topic without even the hint of a transition. I've helped Detective Briggs on a few cases, and yes, I helped out on this one. But since I know the main person of interest, I've been taken off the case. And yes he's single. Not that that has any bearing on this conversation."

"It's probably better that you're not involved. I don't want you anywhere near that monster Jacob if he's killing people left and right."

A long, audible sigh was my way of letting her know it was about time to end the call. "I should get to sleep, Mom. I've got a busy work day tomorrow."

"Oh? Anything special happening in your little flower shop?" She had yet to call my shop by its name, Pink's Flowers, and it was never 'your flower shop' but always 'your *little* flower shop' as if I was running some Barbie sized flower stand outside of the Barbie Dream House.

"It's a *little* holiday event that's rather important in the florist world. You might have heard of it. In fact, I know you've heard of it because you used to leave sticky notes all over Dad's side of the mirror reminding him about your favorite flowers and chocolates."

"Of course, Valentine's Day. That reminds me, I'm behind on those sticky notes. Well, I will let you get your beauty sleep, my darling. And remember stay clear of—"

"Yes, yes, I will try to avoid direct paths with mass murderers, crazy kidnappers and marauding pirates. Actually, scratch that last one. You know how I love pirates, especially the marauding kind."

"Now I really will let you go because you are sounding silly, and you always get silly when you're tired. Good night, sweetums."

"Good night, Mom. Kiss Dad for me."

CHAPTER 28

The last person I expected to see out on Lester's fancy tables was Detective Briggs. He was preoccupied with his notebook while the steam curled up from his coffee cup, taking all the heat with it.

In the early morning, the sunlight fell mostly on the opposite side of the street, so the tables were bathed in the cold shadow of morning.

Briggs looked up from his notes as I approached. "Miss Pinkerton, how are you?" He closed the notebook quickly.

I looked pointedly at it. "I wasn't trying to look at your notes. Besides, I've seen your handwriting, and it takes more than a quick glance to decipher it."

He looked properly embarrassed. "Yes, I agree, but I wasn't actually hiding it from you. What brings you over to the coffee shop?"

I decided not to tell him that I'd seen him when I walked to my door and decided to stop by for a chat. "I was out of coffee. I'm just stopping in to fuel up. I've got a long work day ahead. You do too, I imagine. What with the murder case and all. Not that I'm bringing it up—not to pry but I was just wondering if you had a chance to talk to anyone." I waved my hand. "Probably not. I did just show you the rainbow picture last night."

As I spoke, he had to work harder and harder to suppress a smile. I did like his smile. Is that what I mentioned to my mom and Aunt Sheila? What on earth could I have blurted in my rum-soaked haze that made my mom think there was something going on between Briggs and me? And why was I talking about him while sitting in my mom's living room next to the artificial Christmas tree playing cards with my Aunt Sheila, who had never married but always seemed to have copious amounts of advice about men?

"As a matter of fact, I did get a chance to talk to several people. I went up to Maple Hill last night just to have a look around and check out travel paths and time myself walking between trailers. Autumn, Lydia and Alexander were at the site, bundled up in winter gear, sipping beers and sharing stories about Jasper. A sort of make-shift memorial, I suppose."

"Only those three?" I asked. "My friend Hazel wasn't there? The petite woman with big glasses and bigger blue eyes who moves sort of fast, like a hummingbird?"

"Yes, I know who Miss Bancroft is, but I didn't see her. Just the three I mentioned. They were surprised to see me and probably not too thrilled that I'd interrupted their memorial. I told them I had a few questions for each of them but that it could wait. But as I turned to leave, Miss Harris, the photographer called me back. She then nudged Miss Nola forward. Miss Nola looked reluctant to speak, and I soon found out why. She had extremely important information to add."

"Autumn? What information and why would she keep it to herself?"

Briggs looked down at the coffee cup in his hand. He always

shifted his gaze away from mine when there was something he didn't want to tell me. "Briggs?"

"I believe she kept it to herself because, if true, it's very incriminating for Mr. Georgio."

I shrank down in my coat and scarf at his disappointing words. Briggs always caught any change in my mood. He'd obviously noticed me getting swallowed up by my winter gear.

"I'm sorry to have to tell you that, Lacey." Lately, he dropped the formality in addressing me as Miss Pinkerton, but it always seemed to be when he was apologizing for something. I rarely called him James, and stuck only with Detective Briggs. Mostly because it was his request I did so. Although, I was very fond of the name James, and it suited him well.

I gathered my composure and straightened enough to fill out my puffy winter coat again. "I don't understand. What could Autumn have said? Was it a different motive than jealousy because I would hardly think anything she said on that matter would . . . uh, matter." It seemed I was back in defense mode for Jacob.

"It had nothing to do with motive and more to do with circumstantial evidence, evidence that helps our case against him."

Briggs hadn't invited me to sit, but I climbed up on the stool next to him anyway. "Now that you've mentioned it, I'm not leaving until you tell me. Please," I added, just in case.

"It's not a secret because the others already know. It seemed Lydia had to talk Autumn into telling me. Autumn's trailer is parked between Jasper's and Jacob's. On the day of the murder, after she finished her facial, Autumn went back to her trailer to rest and wait for the work day to start. Jasper was killed sometime between the time she left and an hour later when Alexander found the body. Autumn said she sat down on the bed at the rear corner of the trailer to take off her shoes and she heard someone walk by. She glanced out the window. It was Jacob. She opened the window and called out to him but he ignored her and kept walking."

"Maybe he just didn't hear her."

"It's possible. She was angry at him for ignoring her and slammed closed the window. She fell asleep on the bed until she heard Alexander yelling. She never saw where Jacob went or the time he returned to his own trailer. Through the last two interviews, Jacob stuck tight to his claim that he'd gone to sleep off his illness in his trailer. He claims he didn't wake up until he heard Alexander. Autumn's account contradicts his statement."

Lester popped his head out the door. "Hey, Lacey, can I whip you up a coffee mocha?"

My stomach was not feeling it, and there was a terrible bitter taste in my mouth, left there by the newest revelation in the case. I waved. "No thanks, Les. I drank two cups before I left home."

I realized too late my mistake. Briggs was already giving me a raised brow.

"Yes, I lied. I didn't run out of coffee. I saw you sitting here." I pointed to my shop. "Les and I are neighbors, remember? And I was being nosy. So there you have it. Full confession. But with what you just told me, I'm sort of wishing I wasn't so darn nosy. Maybe I'm better left out in the dark with this case."

"It seems as if you still have feelings for Jacob." He quickly lifted the coffee cup to his mouth as if he wished he hadn't just blurted out that observation.

"You are quite wrong, Detective Briggs. I don't have any special feelings for the man. He left me somewhat broken, after all. I'm just upset because all this time I considered myself to be an excellent judge of character. But it seems I'm no judge at all. I wore the man's ring for a short time. I considered him 'the one' until I discovered that I wasn't the 'only one'. But that hardly would make him capable of murder. Now I don't know if I can ever trust my own judgment again."

Briggs placed his hand over my gloved hand. "We don't know if he is the murderer yet, and his being guilty hardly makes you a bad judge of character. You've helped me solve more than one murder in the past six months. That intuition of yours never fails." It was a sweet attempt to assure me, but I wasn't at all convinced.

I wouldn't confess it to Briggs, but at the time, I fell quite head over heels for Jacob. Jacob, the murderer. Ugh. Now I was being my mom.

I straightened enough to realize that Elsie's tease about a customer falling off the tall stool wasn't too far off. The cold air made the surface slippery and small. I positioned myself more securely in the middle of the seat.

"You're right. Jacob is not guilty yet. Maybe Autumn made the whole thing up. Maybe she was upset with Jacob and decided to make him sweat just a little more about this whole thing. I know the girl, and I wouldn't put it past her."

A few lines creased next to Briggs' mouth, a result of a lopsided, amused grin. "I'm going to be taking her formal statement today. We'll see if she changes it. And I'm going to be talking to Alexander again about the picture." He patted his phone. "It seems he hasn't been forthcoming about the true nature of his relationship with Jasper. No one has, in fact, and I find that troubling." He stepped down from the stool.

I jumped off as well. "You're right. There does seem to be some kind of secret conspiracy surrounding their relationship." I clapped my hands together once. The sound was muted by my gloves, but I had his attention. "What if all three of them are in on the murder, and they want Jacob to take the blame?"

"Motive?" he asked. "And don't forget we're working under the notion that the murderer was strong enough to hold a pillow over Jasper's face."

I opened my mouth to answer him but realized I had no suggestions.

"And ruining Jacob Georgio would probably be an end to the

company and to their careers. Doesn't make much sense for them to sell their employer down the river, as they say."

"Maybe it's just some creepy stranger who—I don't know, but sometimes the killers are an unknown entity, a drifter passing through maybe."

"Yes, I know. It's sort of my business to know stuff like that."

"Yes, right. Just putting it out there."

"Trust me, Miss Pinkerton, we're looking at all the angles. Unfortunately, so far all arrows are pointing to the same suspect. But the case is far from closed."

I nodded weakly. "Thank you for filling me in. Have a good day, Detective Briggs."

"You too, Miss Pinkerton."

CHAPTER 29

$\mathcal{E}$arlier in the morning I was questioning my ability to judge people's characters. Just two hours later, I was heading up to Maple Hill to visit the very person who had me doubting my judgment. Even as my foot pressed down on the pedal to coax my shabby little car up the hill to the Hawksworth Manor, I knew should have swung the car around and headed back down. Hazel had dropped by the shop, but I had been far too busy with customers to spare her any time. She scribbled a few lines on a notepad, then left the shop before we could talk. The message said that she heard Jacob was going to be charged and that he was beside himself with grief. She said he left the hotel early with Baxter Redmond, and they hadn't seen them since.

Once the shop quieted for the morning lull, I slipped next door to the bakery and bought a fudge brownie, Jacob's favorite dessert, and headed up the hill. Jacob had been asked not to leave town, so I deduced that they had gone back up to Maple Hill to check out the scene and search for anything else that might help their case.

I drove up to the top of the hill and parked along the side of the road. The makeshift police blockade had been dismantled, but there was still caution tape up around Jasper's trailer. The Hawksworth house looked extra sad. It seemed to only get attention when there was a tragedy on its grounds. It looked much more stately without the crooked chain link fence propped up around it. I was sure the fence would be replaced soon. The house was just too much of a temptation for curious trespassers. Like me. With everything that had happened, I'd pushed my last trip to the library far back in my mind. Along with the unpleasant meeting with the town's mayor.

Baxter Redmond was still wearing the same toffee brown toupee, but he had more facial hair, namely a thick moustache that had been dyed to match the toffee brown hair piece. He made an attempt to button his coat as he walked toward me. His belly made that impossible. He didn't seem to recognize me, which wasn't too surprising because we'd hardly ever interacted.

"Excuse me, Miss, can I help you?"

"Actually, I was just hoping to see Jacob."

Redmond was puffing some from his brisk walk across the lot. He stopped a few feet away and took out his glasses to get a better look at me. "Miss Pinkerton?"

"Yes. It's me. How are you, Mr. Redmond?"

"Hell of a mess. I understand you and that nose of yours were helping the police frame Jacob."

"What? Frame? No. That's not true." I was about to argue the point when Redmond looked past my shoulder.

"Lacey?" Jacob's voice sounded rough from the cold. Being faced with a murder charge was probably not helping either. The rings under his eyes got darker each time I saw him.

I lifted up the pink bakery box. "It's a fudge brownie, possibly the best fudge brownie in the world."

He smiled weakly as he took the box. "Thanks. Maybe I can just commit chocolate suicide."

"You've delivered your brownie, Miss Pinkerton. But Jacob and I have work to do." Redmond had managed to button his coat, but the fabric was straining to hold hands with itself.

I decided to ignore Redmond and turned to Jacob. "I just came by to see how you were doing."

Jacob nodded. "I've been better. They finally let me back into my trailer. I was just about to go inside and get some aspirin. Come with me and we can talk."

Redmond cleared his throat. "As your legal counsel, I advise against it."

"I think Lacey's already pointed out all the important evidence to the police. I don't think there's much else she can do." Jacob motioned with his head and I followed.

"Glad to see you don't hold a grudge," I noted as we crossed the lot to his trailer.

"This coming from the woman who walked out of my life and never talked to me again because she thought she smelled another woman's perfume on my collar."

I stopped short of the steps to his trailer. "That's because you did have another woman's perfume on your shirt."

His shoulders relaxed with a sigh. "There was a time when that nose of yours worked for me, instead of against me."

I followed him up the steps without a second thought. Maybe it was stupid and dangerous. Or maybe it was because I knew Jacob was not a murderer.

"They combed the place for evidence. I guess they thought I'd have some of that facial mask on my things, but they couldn't find any." Jacob walked to the small refrigerator and put the brownie inside. He made a sound. "I'm really losing my mind," he was speaking into the refrigerator.

"Uh, if you're waiting for your refrigerator to answer, then I might have to agree with you."

He straightened with a can of orange soda. "I have no idea when I grabbed an orange soda from the catering truck."

"You hate orange soda," I pointed out unnecessarily.

"Yes. Why would I have picked one up, and when did I pick it up? See, losing my mind. It's this blasted cold." Then he turned to the long line of cold medicines on the counter and reached for the bottle of aspirin. "I always get sick at the most inconvenient time." For a second he seemed to forget his predicament and the smile that had captured my heart appeared. "Remember that trip to the Bahamas with the board members?"

"How could I forget? You were so sick with the flu and so drowsy on cold medicines, I had to go alone to all the dinners. With five of the stuffiest board members on the planet I might add."

"You were a trooper. They all thought highly of you before the trip, but you really won them over during." His smile faded some. "I'm sorry I hurt you, Lacey. I never got a chance to say that."

"Water under the bridge. Now you've got bigger things to think about. Jacob, why didn't anyone know that Alexander and Jasper were seeing each other?"

He swallowed the aspirin. "How did you know about that?"

I pulled out my phone and showed him the rainbow picture. He stared at it for a long moment. "That must have been just a few hours before he died." And there it was, the thing I was looking for that would convince me that I hadn't misjudged his character, the proof I needed that Jacob was not a murderer. There was no false sympathy or indifference in his words. He was genuinely sad that Jasper was dead.

"The agency that Jasper worked for kept total control of any publicity for their models. They thought Jasper's success as the male face of Georgio's Perfume would be hindered if people knew about his personal life. It was in the contract we signed when we hired Jasper. Redmond and I were just waiting for the agency to release us from the non-disclosure reference. But I'm not sure that will mean anything now." He picked up the pile of empty lozenge wrappers off the counter and tossed them in the trash.

"I heard there was some new evidence."

"Yep, it seems my own people, including my girlfriend, have turned on me. Autumn insists she saw me walk by her trailer around the time of the murder, but I was right here sleeping." He waved his hand over the medicine bottles. "In a cold medicine coma. I can't figure out why she would lie about me."

"So, it is a lie?" I asked.

"Yes. I know you don't have any reason to believe me after what I did to you, but I slept through that entire morning. Right up until the moment I heard Alexander yelling."

"Did Autumn know about Jasper and Alexander?" I asked.

"I'm not sure. She was pretty close with Jasper. They dated, but he had just used her to get into the agency. Still, they hung out all the time. She might have known. I think the flirting game she was playing with Jasper was to upset Alexander. Jasper was angry with him about something. Either way, it doesn't help my case. Redmond is going to drill the detective on motive today to see what angle he's coming from. Or maybe you can give us some insight, since you seem to know him well."

I shook my head. "Nope, I'm off the case."

"Except that you're up here right now, and your eyes have swept this small room a few times since you stepped inside."

I was about to be offended, but he looked so miserable I decided to ignore his insinuation that I was a police plant.

"Speaking of me looking around—" I walked to the coffee table next to his couch. There were no cigarette butts in the ashtray. "I can't help but notice that your ashtray is clean."

"Yes. Wow, you are still obsessed about my dirty ashtray habit."

"No, that's not it." I rolled my eyes. "And even though those cigarettes weren't tobacco, it was a gross habit. But why are they clean?"

He tapped the front of his neck. "Like I told the detective, they were making my throat worse."

"But the one they found in your ashtray on the day of the murder? You said you didn't remember lighting it."

"I still don't. Must have been the cold medicine. Or maybe it's such an automatic habit, I couldn't remember lighting the thing. Or maybe I'm just losing my mind." He shook his head. "I just want to wake up from this terrible nightmare."

Redmond's heavy footsteps sounded on the metal stairs to the trailer. He knocked hard enough to rattle the walls and windows.

"Guess that's my cue to go. I've got to get back to work."

Jacob nodded. "Take care, Lacey. And thanks for the fudge brownie. They're my favorite."

I smiled weakly at him. "I know."

CHAPTER 30

The clove cigarette thing wouldn't rest in my mind. I wasn't exactly sure what I was looking for, but I decided to see if I could talk Briggs into letting me smell the evidence again.

The moment I saw his car drive past the flower shop, I hurried out the door and headed down the sidewalk to the police station. He saw me as he stepped out of his car. He was carrying an evidence bag that seemed to be holding a pair of socks. He made a pathetic attempt to hide the bag by holding it behind him.

"Miss Pinkerton, where are you off to in such a hurry?"

"I was hoping to catch you, and it seems I have."

"I'm actually kind of busy."

"Yes, I saw the evidence bag you are working so hard to hide."

"And doing a terrible job of it, apparently." He pulled the bag out from behind his back.

I stared down at the socks and noted two things, not as an amateur sleuth but as a woman. They were men's socks, and they were dirty as if the wearer had gone hiking in them.

156

"You don't have to tell me," I said.

He nodded once. "That's good because I wasn't going to."

"That's fine." I knew my nostrils were flaring slightly as I said it, but I couldn't stop myself.

"What was it you wanted?" he asked.

We were still standing on the sidewalk which I took as his way of telling me there was no reason to go inside the station. Fortunately, Hilda popped her head out the door. "Lacey, you have to come in and try the sugar cookies I baked."

I shrugged and flashed Briggs a smug grin as I slipped past him to follow Hilda to her plate of sugar cookies. They were in the shape of hearts and covered with red and pink sprinkles.

"Now mind you, they aren't as good as Elsie's but then no one bakes like that woman." Hilda went behind the counter to her desk and grinned proudly as she held the plate up for me. I kept the corner of my eye on Briggs, who'd walked through the gate with his bag of dirty socks. Surprisingly, he paused and watched me take a bite. As my teeth clamped down and the dry, flavorless cookie crumbled over my taste buds, I discovered why he had stopped. He turned his face to hide his amusement, while I worked up an enthusiastic chew and nod over the cookie. Hilda fidgeted with excited anticipation, waiting for my glowing critique. The cookie coated my throat like dry flour, and it took more than a few hard swallows to get the thing down.

I held the other half in my fingers. "I'll save this for later. It's just delicious, and I want to enjoy it after my lunch."

She held up the plate again. "Here take another and take one for Ryder."

"Oh—are you sure?" I picked up two more and winked at her. "So good."

"Miss Pinkerton." Briggs stopped at his office door. "May I speak to you for a moment?"

"Yes," I said on a thankful intake of air. I covered my mouth to stifle a cough caused by a few dry chunks of cookie lodged in my throat as Hilda buzzed me through the gate.

Briggs shut the office door behind me, and without a word, walked to one of the cupboards in his office. He pulled out a bottle of water, untwisted the top and handed it to me.

I lifted it in a silent thank you and washed down the rest of the cookie crumbs. My throat cleared of choking debris, I sighed.

"A little dry," he noted.

"Like the Sahara desert during a drought. I'm not an expert baker, but I think she might have left out everything except the flour. But she's very proud of them."

"I know. I've got my very own plate." Briggs walked to his desk and lifted a napkin on a plate filled with the cookies. He turned around and leaned against the front of his desk. "What were you coming to see me about? And I'm hoping it doesn't have to do with the murder case."

"It has to do with the murder case."

He nodded. "I figured as much."

"It's all for nothing I'm sure, but I just wanted to get a whiff of the clove cigarette one more time."

"Really? Odd request. What do you think you'll find?"

"Nothing. Probably nothing."

Hilda knocked on the door and walked inside with a paper. "Sorry to interrupt but we just got this from the lab." She was still beaming about her cookies. I showed her that I was still holding the little treasures in my hand.

"Silly me, you need a napkin for those." Hilda disappeared and scurried right back with a napkin.

Red and pink sprinkles littered the office floor as I wrapped the cookies in the napkin. Hilda walked out and closed the door behind her.

I turned back around to find Briggs reading the lab work. His brows looked stern as he read down the page. I could only assume it was the lab work from Jasper's autopsy, and I could only assume that they'd found something of interest.

Briggs put the paper down on the desk behind him.

"You don't have to tell me what's in the report."

"All right," he said with that aggravating calmness he was so good at.

I kept my foot from stomping like an angry kid. "No, come on, tell me. Please. I'll keep my lips zipped." I turned the invisible key.

He pushed off from the desk. "It seems that Jasper had a lot of sedative in his blood. It lines up with what his coworkers had told me."

"Yes, Jasper struggled with insomnia."

"It seems so." He put up his hand up to stop my next question. "It wasn't enough for a suicide if that was what you were about to ask. It was still death by suffocation. It just means he was probably out cold when the pillow was pushed down over his face."

I released a disappointed breath. "I see. I just thought maybe . . . Wait. That means that the murderer didn't have to be stronger or bigger than Jasper. It could have been anyone."

"True. But if these socks that I just collected from Jacob's belongings turn out to have the same dirt on them as the soil sample from Maple Hill, I think we have our 'anyone'."

"Socks? Now this I know for certain. Jacob Georgio would not go walking around outside in socks. Especially not when he's sick."

"Except that the witness, namely, Miss Nola, noted that in her official statement. When she saw Jacob walk past her trailer, he was only wearing socks. No shoes. She thought it was odd too."

"This just keeps getting more impossible to believe." I tilted my head politely. "Can I please just run Samantha past that cigarette again?"

His confusion cleared quickly. "That's right. I forgot you settled on a name for your partner." He tapped the side of his own nose.

"Actually, I believe you came up with it, comparing my nose

twitch to Samantha on Bewitched. If only I could produce a little magic with that twitch. Then I'd erase this whole week from the calendar."

Briggs checked his watch. It was one of those chrome and black sporty man watches that looked extremely nice on his wrist. "I've got ten minutes. Let's go to the evidence room."

"Really?" In my excitement, I crushed the dry cookies in the napkin. We both watched as crumbs cascaded onto the floor. "Oops." I walked to his desk and grabbed the napkin off his plate of cookies and wrapped it as a second layer around the broken cookies in my napkin. "There. Hilda won't know the difference."

I followed Briggs to the evidence room, a stale smelling, utilitarian room that was kept cold to preserve evidence.

"Brrr, I hope I can even smell in this icy atmosphere."

"Do you want to skip it?"

"No, continue. This will only take a second."

He carried the bag with the clove cigarette over to the exam table and handed me the latex gloves. I shoved my napkin full of cookie dust into my coat pocket and pulled on the thin plastic gloves.

"What exactly are you looking for?" Briggs asked as he pulled on his own gloves.

"I'm not totally sure."

He unzipped the bag and reached in for the clove cigarette. The brand Jacob smoked were thin and black with a tiny red band near the mouth end. I took it gently between my fingers. The end had been lit but very little of it had been smoked, if any. It seemed highly probable that Jacob had, out of habit, lit the cigarette, taken one good puff and been quickly reminded that his throat was too raw to smoke.

I ran the cigarette past my nose. With something as fragrant as cloves, it would be hard to smell anything else. But then my hypersomia had earned me a hefty amount of respect in the perfume industry for the very reason that I was able to discern many scents from one bottle of perfume. The cold room and the curious gaze of the man standing next to me made it hard to concentrate. I closed my eyes and twitched my nose to wake up my highly sensitive olfactory receptor cells. I moved the cigarette beneath my nose as if I was breathing in the fragrance from a glass of wine. I could smell the clove and the singed end of the cigarette and possibly one other earthy scent. Most likely another compound in the cigarette. But the thing that was most interesting to me was the scent that was conspicuously absent. "Menthol," I said succinctly.

"Menthol." Briggs immediately reached for his notebook. He flipped it open and clicked his pen. "You smell menthol." He began writing before I could answer.

"No, I don't smell any menthol."

Briggs peered up at me and started to scratch out what he'd written.

"No, don't cross that out. Just add a big *no* to the front of it. Because there is *no* menthol smell."

His stubble covered jaw moved back and forth in a sort of impatient fashion. "I suppose I could start a list of all the smells that aren't on the cigarette, but I've only got a few minutes."

"You won't need to. Menthol is the only important absent smell."

It always took him a few minutes to catch up to my line of thinking. I could see a metaphorical light bulb turn on over his dark head of hair. "The throat lozenges. Jacob eats those things like candy."

"Right. And he was taking them before the murder because I ran into him outside the Corner Market on Monday. If he had lit that cigarette, I'm sure I would smell the menthol from his lozenges on the end. But I don't." I handed him the cigarette to return to the bag.

"Miss Pinkerton, before you get too excited about your latest revelation, don't forget there is other evidence that still points to Jacob. And as hard as it is to connect concrete evidence together to solve a crime, it's much harder to use evidence that should have been there to solve it. If that makes sense."

"It does. I guess our minds are still synching up like a couple of seasoned partners."

He shook his head but with a smile.

"I'm just going to keep this nugget locked up in my mind. You never know when it will come in handy." I looked back toward the shelf where the rest of the evidence for the case was stored and looked back at him with a pleading grin.

He started his defense before I even got the question out. "You said the cigarette. And I have work to do."

"Just two seconds with the pillow. That's all. Two sniffs. Two seconds."

A low grunt followed as he acquiesced , it seemed, against his better judgment. He walked with extra hard steps to the shelf and pulled down the pillow. He pointed to the box of gloves. "New ones so there's no cross contamination."

"Make sense." I pulled off the first pair and dropped them in the trash can. Then I stuck my hands into the second pair. They were a perfect fit for his hands but my fingers were swimming in them. I held up my wrinkly hand. "Definitely couldn't do surgery in these. They'd likely slip right off and end up in some body cavity." I laughed at my joke, but Briggs had a decidedly less amused reaction.

He pulled the pillow sharply from its bag. "Two seconds and I'm starting now with *one*."

I grabbed the pillow and pressed my face close to it. The front side or the murder side was stained with the pink clay mask that Jasper had been wearing. Most of the substance had dried and some of it had fallen off, leaving behind a powdery residue. The killer would have had to hold both edges of the pillow. I ran my nose along the trim of the pillow. My heart sank as once again I recognized the distinct scent of Jacob's cologne. I turned the pillow over and as my nose raced over the fabric to the other side, I detected an odor, the same earthy odor I'd smelled on the cigarette. I couldn't quite place it. I didn't know all the compounds they put in clove cigarettes, but something about it was familiar.

Briggs held out his hand. "Two."

I handed him the pillow.

"Anything significant?" he asked.

I shook my head. "No, unfortunately."

He put the pillow away and back in its place on the evidence shelf, then walked me out. "Miss Pinkerton, try not to get yourself in a knot about this. We'll get it sorted out, and the real murderer will face his . . . or her . . . day in court."

I walked out with heavy steps feeling more depressed than ever.

"Let me know what Ryder thinks of the cookie," Hilda called as I walked through the gate.

CHAPTER 31

"If it's all right, boss, I'm going to take pictures of the Valentine's bouquets and post them on Instagram."

"Good idea." I finished washing the potting soil off my hands.

Ryder carried his three Valentine bouquet examples to the island. Kingston, aware that something riveting would be happening in the center of the store, lifted off his perch and caused a black feathered ruckus during the short flight to the work island.

"I'll lure him back to his perch with some seeds." I hurried over to grab the coffee can of crow treats.

"No, wait. I think having a tame crow in the picture will get more likes." As soon as he suggested it, Kingston pulled a rose leaf off with his beak. More petals fluttered down behind it. Ryder laughed.

"Are you sure you don't want me to move my pushy bird?"

"Nope, I'm sure. I'll try and get one with him eating a rose petal. In fact . . ." Ryder picked up a fallen petal. Kingston's head turned left and right with interest as Ryder placed the red petal on top of the crow's shiny black head. He quickly snapped a picture before

Kingston realized he was wearing his favorite edible flower like a hat. He puffed up and gave his feathers a good shake, dislodging the treat right where he needed it—at his feet.

"I'm going to go into the office to place some orders. Let me know if Kingston gets too obnoxious."

"We'll be fine."

I sat down at the computer. The early morning visit with Jacob and then the follow-up visit with Briggs still had gears spinning in my head. It seemed impossible to think that the cigarette wouldn't have the smell of menthol on it with the way Jacob had been sucking those lozenges down for his sore throat. It was as if he'd somehow lit the thing without actually putting it in his mouth.

I spent twenty minutes on mind-numbing paperwork to help me kick all the other thoughts from my head. Surprisingly, it had helped. I was in full office mode and picked up my list for a purchase order when Ryder called down the hallway.

"I posted some pictures on Instagram. Check them out and see what you think. The ones with Kingston are already racking up likes."

I picked up my phone and scrolled through the images. I beamed like a proud mom at the picture of Kingston standing with his black eyes peering out from a wall of yellow and white daisies. "These are great," I yelled back to him. "My bird is a ham," I yelled again just as Ryder came around the corner. "Oh sorry, didn't know you were right there. I love these. You are a talented photographer. And I think my bird has a future in modeling."

Ryder laughed. "I agree. Hey, I'm going to head out for the day. I'll open tomorrow."

"Sounds good. See you in the morning. Oh, wait."

Ryder's face popped back into the doorway. "Yeah?"

"I'll be a little late tomorrow. I nearly forgot that my neighbor, Dash, is taking me on a flight along the coast."

Ryder stepped into the office as he pushed his long bangs away from his rounded eyes. "What? How cool. Lucky you."

"I'm excited and a little nervous too. I've never been in a small, two seat plane. But it should be fun, and my phone shows nice weather. I don't want to keep you. I'll be here before noon tomorrow."

"Have fun." I heard Ryder thanking Kingston for his help while he pulled on his coat and gloves. A few seconds later, the door opened and shut.

The pleasant diversion had swept my mind off work and the void was immediately filled by the investigation. The one person who I hadn't given enough thought about was Jasper. I'd been so caught up in trying to find reasons why Jacob wasn't the murderer, I'd given little thought to the poor victim, in this case a vibrant, talented man who had a stunning future in front of him. I was never close with Jasper, and he could be arrogant and self-centered on occasion. Still, it was wrong not to give him some considera-tion. I remembered that he had a very active and sometimes enter-taining Instagram account.

I searched for Jasper's profile and his pictures popped up. It felt a little eerie looking at his pictures and posts, especially the selfies where he looked extremely happy and alive. Most of the pictures and posts were of friends and himself, a short narrative of his life cut way too short. My thumb rolled the next row of pictures up. I was about to move on when a familiar face caught my eye. It was Hazel. She was behind her desk located outside of Jacob's office. She was concentrating deeply on a report. It was easy to know that she was unaware Jasper was taking the picture because the poor woman had her finger in her nose. Jasper's comment read; Hazel showing us all how to multitask. The picture had well over two hundred thousand likes.

I put down the phone. It felt as if all the energy drained out of me at once. I had never seen the picture, but I could only imagine how hurt and embarrassed Hazel had been. She was someone who put a great deal of importance on people liking her and thinking well of her. It must have been nothing short of devastating. It made me feel a touch less guilty about not giving Jasper enough thought. It had truly been an evil stunt.

I hadn't seen Hazel since Thursday. I felt bad about not having more time to spend with her. I'd even brushed her off briskly several times. I picked up the phone and texted her to see if she wanted to meet for some coffee. I had no plans to bring up the picture. I just wanted to be a more supportive friend. The picture incident happened after I'd left Georgio's. Which was fortunate for Jasper because if I had been there I would have given him a large piece of my mind. It was disappointing to think that Jacob hadn't stepped in to tell Jasper to delete the picture. Although, it was entirely possible Jacob didn't even know about it. He was never big on social media, and Hazel was most likely too ashamed to bring it up to him. There I was again, working hard to defend Jacob.

Hazel's text came right back. "I can be there in twenty."

"Sounds good." Maybe Hazel would have new updates on the investigation.

CHAPTER 32

The moment I'd finished firming up the coffee date with Hazel, I had a small rush of customers. I texted Lester and the wonderful man was kind enough to deliver two of his special cinnamon lattes.

Lester, who rarely ever seemed to be cold, was wearing one of his signature Hawaiian shirts, a bright turquoise and yellow number that looked wholly out of place in the dead of winter but looked completely right on Lester. The only concession for the cold weather was a thin, long sleeve shirt that he'd put on beneath the summery shirt.

I had just finished up with my last customer as he placed the two coffees on the island. "Two of my cinnamon spice lattes. I topped them with whipped cream and cinnamon candy hearts. I put them on your tab."

"You're the best."

Lester looked around. "Don't tell me the crow is drinking lattes now. That bird really does think he's human."

"He does, but even I draw the line at letting him drink coffee.

He's snarky enough as it is without caffeine." Kingston cawed loudly and shook his wings as if he knew we were talking about him.

I decided not to wait for my first sip. "Hmm, so good and spicy. How's Elsie? I haven't seen her today."

Lester leaned his forearm on the counter. "Between you and me, she's gotten herself in a bit of a bind with that ridiculous flyer and that British actor. I don't know what she was thinking."

I looked sternly at him. "Uh, you don't? Couldn't have anything to do with that extravagant table set up you've got going in front of the Coffee Hutch?"

"I bought furniture. She told the world that a famous actor was coming to have tea and cookies with them on Valentine's Day. Now who's going over the edge on this? My sister or me?"

I took another sip of coffee to let him know I was staying out of the sibling table war.

Lester laughed. "Guess that's what they call 'saved by the latte'. Well, I need to get back to the shop. It's a slow afternoon, so I started the task of sanitizing all the counters. Now that I've started, I've got to finish, otherwise the un-sanitized half will contaminate the clean half and I'll have to start from square one."

"Thanks for the delivery service."

Lester stopped and held the door open for Hazel who swept in with far less aplomb than usual. In fact, she looked depressed with a sullen expression and a slow paced walk.

I reached for her coffee and held it up, assuming she needed it. As I pulled back my elbow, I sent Ryder's basket of dried sage clusters to the floor. It turned out not that many people were into the holistic properties of burning dried sage.

"Enjoy while I scoop up the mess." I stooped down with the basket and picked up the clusters. I stood up. Hazel was taking a long sip of the coffee. I used the time to zip over and wash my hands. Otherwise my coffee would taste like sage instead of cinnamon. Fortunately dried sage wasn't nearly as fragrant as fresh.

I headed back over to the stools where Hazel had perched herself with her latte. I joined her on the next stool.

"What's wrong? You look rather glum. Although, I'm not sure I can take another bout of bad news."

Hazel took another long drink from the coffee and sighed at the end of it. "No news. I guess the events of the week are finally catching up to me." She touched her throat. "Plus, I think I'm getting Jacob's cold."

"That's awful. Feeling down and being sick on top of it." That statement took me back to poor Jacob. What a week he was having. "You'll need to get better fast. You've got big life changes happening soon."

Hazel's blue eyes rounded with confusion.

"Your new job? I guess this wasn't the best way to end your career at Georgio's. Do you know what your official tasks will be at Tremaine's?"

Rather than answer, she picked up her coffee and drank some more. Just like the move I'd made to evade Lester's question.

She placed the empty cup down. "Gosh, I've hardly given it any thought with all this craziness. I think I'll be in accounting or marketing possibly."

"Those are such vastly different departments. I thought you told me you were going to be an administrative assistant, a parallel job to the one you have now. But I guess I misheard that."

"Yes, it seems so."

What it seemed was that there was nothing normal about our coffee date. Hazel was always peppy and chatty, but today, I had to pull information out of her. And I was certain I hadn't misheard her when she first told me about her new job. The new job would be such a stark change in her otherwise very uniform life, it was hard to believe that she wasn't thinking about it all the time. Even with the *craziness*.

I wasn't sure which way to steer the conversation, since Hazel wasn't doing any steering on her own. "How is everyone?"

"As well as can be expected." Hazel unzipped her warm winter coat. She was still wearing the brightly colored sweater underneath. "We're all waiting for permission to leave town. We're stuck in the middle of this. From what I heard this morning, from Lydia, it won't be long before they bring charges against Jacob. Then we can go home and wait to be called as witnesses." She said it all so plainly as if she was just talking about a trip to the store instead of her boss of many years being arrested for murder. The entire coffee date had started to unsettle me.

I decided to veer off the subject. "Guess what I'm doing tomorrow? I'm going on my first flight in a small plane. My neighbor is a pilot, and he's flying me along the coast. He promised we could fly right over my house so I could get an aerial view. Of course, I'll probably fret when I see how badly I've let the landscaping go during these cold winter months."

The topic change had helped. A more usual and perky expression returned to her face. "That would be so exciting. But a little scary."

"That pretty much sums up my feelings about it too. I'm somewhat apprehensive, but at the same time, it just seems like too much of an adventure to pass up."

"Your life was always filled with adventure. I envy that, Lacey. And then when you'd had enough of Georgio's and Jacob, you just put on your walking boots and you walked right out of there. And look at this shop. It's so wonderful."

"Well, you'll be going on an adventure too. I'll bet your parents are going to miss you terribly when you move out. I know my parents would love for me to move within walking distance or even driving distance, for that matter. But once I moved away, they started doing a lot more things, like vacations, and they have more friends now. I guess I needed to let them leave the parents' nest."

Hazel laughed but even her laugh seemed off. It seemed she just wasn't herself. Everybody had days like that. I was somewhat relieved when two customers came in. Our coffee date felt clumsy and forced. I'd caught Hazel on an off day. I couldn't blame her for having one. The week had started with a stunning tragedy and had gotten progressively worse. I was sure it was just that the initial shock had worn off and the grim reality had taken hold. It was a normal sequence of emotions for such a catastrophic series of events.

This time I didn't need to hint that I needed to get back to work and that our chat time was over.

Hazel stepped down from the stool. "Thanks so much for the coffee, Lacey. Have fun tomorrow. I hope we can see each other at least once more before we leave town."

"Let's make a point of it, Hazel."

CHAPTER 33

*M*y fingers gripped the edges of the seat. I felt like a kid again on my first real roller coaster ride. It was that mix of thrill, terror and queasiness that made fast rides so much fun. The small plane rattled and wobbled as its tires raced along the runway making the heavy earphones on my head slip forward. I pushed them back. The entire adventure might have been a touch less glamorous than it had been in my imagination, but it was still fun to watch a serious faced Dash, with his official looking black sunglasses and pilot's headset, as he lifted the plane up into the air.

"Whoo!" I said involuntarily, like a sneeze or a cough.

Dash glanced over for a second, then returned his attention to the wide blue stretch of sky in front of us. "Are you all right?" His voice sounded tinny as it came through the earphones. I'd forgotten that I had a microphone sitting in front of my mouth.

"Yep, I'm good."

I could see the tiniest grin form behind his microphone. "It'll be more fun when you finally release your death grip on the seat."

"Yep," I repeated and squeezed the seat edge tighter. The round roofed hangars at the tiny municipal airport fell away along with the rooftops, trees and fields of the town. It was early and the sun was mostly behind us, but the royal blue ocean sparkled with tiny sapphires as the morning light reflected off of it.

I took a few breaths and peeled my fingers off the seat. Just then, the wing on my side dipped down and the plane tilted, sending my hands back to the seat edge. A low, deep laugh rumbled through the headphones. I looked at my pilot.

Dash smiled while staring straight ahead. "Sometimes it takes a few minutes to relax."

The plane leveled out. We buzzed along the coast, and I released my death grip on the seat. It was sort of comical to think that holding tightly to the seat would somehow save me in the unfortunate event that the plane nosedived toward earth. That line of reasoning helped me place my hands in my lap.

I gazed out the window. The scenery didn't blur by, like in a fast moving car. Rather, it meandered past, allowing me to see more details from a decidedly different angle than usual. The nose of the plane was pointing north, inland from the ocean. The land below looked like a giant patchwork quilt of varying shades of green and brown. The trees were still lacking foliage, giving me an even clearer view of the neighborhoods and shops below.

I moved the microphone closer to my mouth. "I can't believe how much detail I can see. In a jet, everything fades away into one gray mass."

"We're cruising at about half the altitude of a commercial jet. Hold on."

It took me a second to comprehend his last comment. I grabbed the seat again as the plane dipped down on my side, and we circled out toward the ocean. I could see the white caps on the waves. Farther from shore, where there was less agitation in the tide, I could see through the emerald glass water to dark shadows swimming beneath the surface.

"Are those sharks?" I asked.

"No, that water's too cold. Dolphins, I think."

I found myself captivated by the sea below. I had never seen it from above. It looked incredibly vast and endless. "It's like an entirely different world down there."

Dash pointed ahead through the front windshield. In the distance, sitting in the midst of a few light clouds, was the spire of the Pickford Lighthouse.

"It's looks tall and majestic from this vantage point. A tall, proud symbol of Port Danby's past." I smiled over at him. "Thank you for inviting me along this morning."

"Thank you for joining me. I feel like I'm seeing everything through a new pair of eyes. Yours. And they are beautiful, I might add."

It was plenty cold in the cramped cockpit, but that didn't stop the heat from rising in my cheeks at his compliment.

"Can we fly over our houses? I want to see an aerial view of my humble little home." Due to the ambient noise in the cockpit, I was talking louder than necessary. But I couldn't seem to stop myself.

"We're heading that direction. I'll drop down lower, so you can get a better view."

My stomach did the elevator lurch as the plane dropped to a lower altitude. Everything below came into much sharper view. I could see a woman on a Mayfield sidewalk walking two dogs. The woman shielded her eyes and looked up to the sky to see what was flying overhead.

"Will she see me if I wave?"

"You can see her way better than she can see you." Dash pointed. "Look out your window. Hawksworth Manor is coming into view next."

"Great. I forgot all about the manor." I kept my focus on the scene outside my window. Maple Hill looked different coming up from the backside. The slope was more gentle and the landscape on the back of the hill was overgrown and wild.

The overhead view of the dilapidated Hawksworth estate was far different than it would have been just last week. The six trailers and trucks from Georgio's Perfume were still parked in a long parade of vehicles from the front edge of the property to the rear. As I swept my eyes past the collection of work vehicles, a bright blue color caught my eye. Feeling much more at ease, I leaned closer to the window to get a better view below.

"It's Hazel!" I said excitedly.

"Who?"

"A friend. She bought a really wild blue sweater from Mod Frock. The blue caught my eye." I kept my focus below. Hazel was unlocking a door to one of the trailers. I reviewed a quick map of the site in my head. It was Jacob's trailer. The bright blue sweater disappeared inside. I sat back. "Interesting," I muttered to myself, forgetting that I was connected to a microphone that was, in turn, connected to Dash.

"What's interesting?" he asked.

"Oh, nothing. I just can't believe how well I can see down to the town." I sat up higher. "Is that my house?"

"Yep."

I sat back again. "I need to position my sprinklers better. I've got way too many brown spots on my lawn."

"The snow did just melt. And spring is around the corner. It's going to be fifteen degrees warmer today than yesterday."

"I'm looking forward to a rise in temperature. But I need to get my tail out to the front yard and do some serious pruning and gardening. I'm looking forward to warmer weather . . . and bicycle rides . . . and shorts with sandals."

"Here, here on that last one." I couldn't see his eyes behind the black sunglasses, but I was sure I detected a wink.

He was darn handsome, and to go with that winning smile and charm, the man was an interminable and, I suspected, an indiscriminate flirt.

CHAPTER 34

$\mathcal{T}$he airport where I'd met Dash for the flight was inland about fifteen miles north of Mayfield. As I headed back to Port Danby, a voice in my head told me to turn off and visit Jacob at the hotel. I had no idea if he was actually at the hotel, but it was hardly out of my way. A few questions had been swirling through my head after I saw Hazel and her sweater that was bright enough to see from space. I'm sure none of the questions were of much importance, but since I'd been left mostly out in the cold on the investigation, I decided to satisfy my own curiosity before it chewed away at the rest of my work day. It was the Saturday before Valentine's Day and I expected it to be busy.

I parked my car in the hotel lot. I sent Jacob a quick text. "I was hoping to talk to you. I'm at the hotel."

The heavy headset had left me with semi-helmet hair. I quickly brushed my hair while I waited for him to answer.

Jacob's text came back. "Sure. Redmond had some calls to make. I've got some time. Room 303."

I climbed out of the car and walked through the lobby to the elevator. A flurry of weekend travelers were checking in. Jacob's room was right next to a fake fern outside the elevator. The Mayfield Hotel was nice, but in Jacob's five star world it would be considered shabby. Maybe he'd grown less spoiled. He hadn't even booked himself the finer room of suites on the top floor.

Jacob opened the door before I knocked. His face had more color and his nose had less.

"You look better." I swept past him into the room.

"Yes but I'm thinking of still downing the cold medicine. I kind of like the haze it puts me in. I do less thinking in that fog."

"That medicine has always affected you worse than others. I remember my theory that you were allergic to the stuff." I turned to him as he shut the door and walked into the room.

He swept his arm around. He had clothes draped on chairs and across the foot of the bed. "Have a seat, if you can find one. I've been turning housekeeping away. I don't want to see people. Especially not the group of people I traveled here with, who have now turned on me."

I stayed standing. "Looks like I just walked into a pity party. And I forgot to bring a gift for the host. You've really got the heat cranked up in here." I unzipped my coat but left it on. I wasn't planning to stay longer than it took for a few quick questions.

"I was trying to sweat the cold out of me."

"Maybe you should think about getting those tonsils out, after all."

"I don't think it'll matter with where I'm going."

"*And* I forgot my tiny violin," I added. "Has Detective Briggs talked about charging you?"

His head moved halfway between a nod and a shake. "Just a matter of time. Says he's having some more lab work done first. The man has it out for me."

"Who? Detective Briggs? Nonsense. He's an honorable, smart man with a great deal of integrity."

Jacob grinned wryly as he walked to the nightstand. "That was a strong, impassioned defense." He picked up his pack of clove cigarettes and pulled one out.

"You're obviously still drunk on cold medicine if you can label that impassioned. And if you're going to light that thing, at least wait until I'm gone."

"That's right. I forgot about that million dollar sensitive nose. The nose that just pushed me into the worst week of my life." He put the clove cigarette back in the box. "Why did you come here today?"

"Wow, you are feeling better. Some of those traits that made it easy for me to walk out of your life are now on full display. I came here hoping to help. But maybe you should just keep drinking that cold medicine."

I turned to leave.

"No wait, Lacey. I'm sorry. I'm just on edge." He laughed weakly. "Withdrawals from antihistamines."

"You're the only man I know who can always find an excuse for being irritating. But I'll give you this one since you're going through a lot. And you have had an excessive amount of medicine. We both know that makes you a little strange." I straightened with a breath as it struck me like a bolt of lightning.

Jacob caught my change in posture. "What's wrong?"

"The Bahamas. The cold medicine. Remember when you walked out onto the beach in the middle of the night? You had no recollection. Just a ton of sand in your room and bed."

"Yes, we figured out I was sleepwalking. My mom told me I used to do it all the time when I was a kid. Especially when I was—"

"Sick," I finished for him. "Then you take medication, and the next thing you know you're walking in your sleep and not remembering a thing."

His face smoothed as he truly comprehended my meaning. "I

was sleepwalking when Autumn saw me. That's why I can't remember a thing. That's why there was an orange soda in the refrigerator. I must have sleepwalked to the catering tables and grabbed an orange soda."

"In your socks."

Jacob was the liveliest I'd seen him since he got to Port Danby. "I'd forgotten just how brilliant you are, Lacey."

"Thank you."

"I'll go next door and tell Redmond right now."

"He'll no doubt tell you that sleepwalking is a weak alibi. I'll let Detective Briggs know that I can confirm that you do sleepwalk. Not sure if it will help or not. Before you go to Redmond, Jacob, I wanted to ask you something else."

"Anything."

"Does Hazel have a key to your trailer?"

The question came out of left field, and it threw him for a second. "I don't know. I didn't give her one specifically, but I guess she might have one. Why?"

"Just wondering. Today I went on a plane ride in a friend's small two seat Cessna. We flew over the coast and over Maple Hill and the manor. Dash, the pilot, dropped the plane low enough so I could see more of the ground below. I saw that bright blue sweater she's been wearing. Hazel was going inside your trailer. Why would she be going in there?"

He scratched his unshaven jaw. "Hmm I'm not sure. I didn't ask her to go inside for anything. But she might have needed some paperwork or something."

"Makes sense." I was almost relieved by his answer. I hated to think that sweet, little Hazel had anything to do with the murder. Hazel had asked me not to bring up her leaving the company to Jacob, in his misery, but he looked less miserable. I was still holding on to a strand of suspicion. "Boy, I guess you'll miss Hazel when she's gone."

He moved his shoulders with a weak shrug.

"What? I thought Hazel was the office dynamo. Whenever anyone needed something, Hazel was the person to see."

"She'd lost her edge in the past year. Her mind was definitely not on the job. I wasn't all that surprised when she turned in her notice. I think she was still hurt that she'd been passed up for a promotion to office manager. She was sure the job would be hers, but there were some awesome applicants. Frankly, Hazel didn't even make the top three."

"Poor Hazel. She must have been devastated. Still, her new job at Tremaine's sounds exciting."

Profound confusion crossed his face. "Tremaine's? She didn't get the job at Tremaine's. That was partially my fault too. My letter of recommendation wasn't exactly glowing. Robert Tremaine and I play golf occasionally. I didn't want to lie on the letter and have it ruin our friendship."

"Oh, Jacob." I couldn't hide the disappointment in my tone. "Hazel has been your most devoted assistant. Couldn't you have flowered up the language some to make it more abstract? You know, like a college midterm essay where you kind of know the answer but all the important details are missing."

He gave me a 'seriously' look. "But that college essay doesn't come back to bite you on the—on the golf course."

"Fair enough. I wonder why Hazel would lie to me?"

"She probably figured you'd hear that she left the company. She wanted to make it seem like she was moving on to bigger and better things. Far as I know, she'll be unemployed."

"Now I'm feeling depressed about Hazel. She's been putting on such a brave face. But it explains why every time I brought up the job at Tremaine's she looked kind of confused. Anyhow, I've got to open up the shop. Let Redmond know that if he needs a statement about your sleepwalking habit, I'd be happy to tell him what I know."

"Thanks for stopping by, Lacey. After my socks came back with matching soil samples from the murder site, I was starting to really fear for my sanity. I don't know why I didn't think of it."

I opened the door and smiled back at him. "Because you were tipsy on cold medicine. Lay off that hard stuff. It's ruined plenty of people's lives."

He laughed as I walked out. I'd always liked his laugh.

CHAPTER 35

*R*yder was pouring water into the three Valentine's arrangements in the front, staring absently out the window as I pulled off my coat and put away my things.

"Everything all right?" I asked.

I'd pulled him from his thoughts. "Huh?" He gave his head a shake. "Yes, fine. We had another twelve orders."

"Wonderful. I'll tally them up and make sure we have everything we need." As I spoke, he seemed to have drifted back to his daydream. It seemed to be an unhappy one at that.

I decided not to pry. But he just didn't seem himself.

"I broke it off with Cherise," he said suddenly.

"I'm sorry to hear that, Ryder. What happened?"

He walked back from the window. "She was trying to control me too much. Telling me when and where and what I should do. I need someone who's a free spirit like me."

My gaze drifted across the street to Lola's Antiques where Lola was moving antique chairs around in a sidewalk display. She had a black bowler pulled down over her red curls and she was wearing her favorite vintage Led Zeppelin t-shirt. I was still convinced Ryder and Lola were right for each other. But I had promised myself to stay out of it.

"Well, I'm here now, Ryder. If you need to take the rest of the day off, feel free."

"I might leave around noon. Some of my friends are heading out on a whale watching cruise. The weather's so nice today, I thought I might join them."

"Perfect." I picked up the folder that was nearly bursting with Valentine's orders. As I lifted it, one of the order sheets slipped out and drifted to the ground, landing right near the trash can. I leaned over to pick it up and got a strong whiff of sage. Apparently, Ryder had given up on his sage bundles. He'd thrown them all away.

My nose filled with the scent again. "That's it," I muttered to myself. "That's the earthy smell on the cigarette."

"Uh oh," Ryder said as I was still kneeled behind the island. "He's back and he still looks upset."

"Who is that?" I asked as I leaned farther under the island to retrieve the order.

The goat bell clanged extra loud.

"She's still not back?" Detective Briggs' urgent, loud voice filled the store.

I popped up from behind the counter.

His jaw had been tight with worry, but it slowly relaxed when he saw me. "Lacey." There was a perceptible drop of his shoulders as he said my name. "You're here."

I looked around. "It *is* my shop."

The few seconds of what I could only read as relief on his face morphed to something harsher. "What on earth were you thinking, Lacey?" It was a tone I'd never heard before. He wasn't even trying to call me Miss Pinkerton. And he was using far more arm gestures than usual. In short, Briggs was anything but his usual cool, smooth as cream self. "It was reckless of you. Those small planes are dangerous and then the pilot—" He scoffed. "Don't even get me started on the pilot."

"I won't because that subject always ends up turning into an argument, and it seems we are about to enter one without even bringing up Dash. How did you know I went on a plane ride?"

His face turned toward Ryder.

Ryder hesitantly raised up his hand. "In my defense, I didn't know it was a secret."

"It wasn't and you're not the one who needs to apologize, Ryder." I turned back to Briggs.

Briggs tapped his chest. "Who me? I have no apology to offer."

"Think I'll just head next door for a coffee," Ryder muttered as he hurried out the door.

"You come barging in here lecturing me and telling me I'm reckless, and you don't feel the slightest bit inclined to apologize?"

That wonderfully masculine jaw of his shifted side to side, pretending to mull it over. "Nope," he said with a firm shake of the head. "No inclination. You should apologize to me."

I laughed. "Now that's rich. Why should I apologize?"

His features softened as he stepped toward the island. His dark gaze held mine for a moment. "Because I've been worried sick. I've hardly gotten a lick of work done all morning. All I could think about was you up there in a rattling old tin can with —never mind."

I stuck the rogue order back into the folder and smiled at him. "You were worried about me?"

"I've got more than a few gray hairs, and I could swear they weren't there before you moved into town. I'm just glad your feet are back on solid ground. Now maybe I can get some work done." He turned to leave.

"Wait. I have some interesting details that I think might help the case."

"Of course you do. So glad you're steering clear of the whole thing."

I held up my hands in surrender. "No crime in talking to old friends."

"And ex-boyfriends," he added.

"Jeez, when something gets stuck in your craw, you just don't let it go." I came around to his side of the island. "First of all, this might sound like a stretch but Jacob sleepwalks when he's had too much cold medicine. I've witnessed it firsthand. Strike that. That's not altogether true. We were on a vacation in the Bahamas with some of the board members."

"Nice."

"Yes, well, Jacob was a catch before he was no longer a catch. But that's not the point. He was sick for most of the vacation."

"He does seem to be rather delicate."

"Yes, I see that now that I'm on the outside of his world. It's easy to overlook things when you think you're in love."

"Think?"

I huffed in aggravation. "Are you going to heckle me through this entire story?"

"Nope, I'm done. Go ahead."

"Jacob was taking a lot of cold medicine, and it made him extra groggy. He woke up one morning and his bed and hotel room were filled with a bunch of unexplained sand. All indications were that he had been sleepwalking out on the beach. Apparently, it was something he did a lot as a kid."

"I suppose that's what the lawyer is coming to see me about today."

"I'm sure of it. Oh, and I nearly forgot, because of the way you entered the store ranting and raving."

"I don't rant and I hardly ever rave." He had returned to the calm, cool detective I knew so well.

"Right. Anyhow, when I did the second smell check on the

cigarette and the pillow I smelled a faint earthy scent. I didn't bring it up because I couldn't really tell what it was. I figured it might have been a natural scent from the cigarette. But now I know it was sage, dried sage to be exact."

He waited for a longer explanation to go with it.

"Ryder was trying to sell bunches of dried sage. It's supposed to have a calming effect on nerves. He probably should've handed you a bundle this morning," I interjected and continued quickly before he could respond. "I've got a wild theory about how the smell got on the cigarette and pillow, but I don't want to share it quite yet. I need to pull together a few more details."

"All right, just as long as you stay out of the investigation." Sarcasm dripped from his words.

"I'm staying on the outside. You stay on the inside. And maybe we'll meet in the middle."

He seemed amused by my plan, but he didn't oppose it. "I'm waiting on some lab results that I think might lead to a charge today."

"Oh really?"

"And I have you to thank for that."

"Oh dear, what have I done now?" I asked.

"Your last inspection of the cigarette got me thinking. We'd found it in Mr. Georgio's trailer and just assumed it belonged to him. But when you mentioned the absence of menthol, I decided to have it checked for DNA. His employees, who are anxious to get back to the city now, were all very willing to have their cheek's swabbed in case his didn't match. All of them except one, that is."

"Let me guess, Hazel Bancroft?"

His eyes widened. "Yes, how did you know?"

"Lucky hunch."

Briggs shook his head. "Your hunches are never just hunches, but as you said, hopefully we'll meet peacefully in the middle on this one." He cast me a more stern look. "Just remember what

188

happened the last time you approached the murderer on your own."

A tiny shiver ran through me as it always did when I thought about the last case we worked on where I nearly became a victim. "I will tread carefully this time. Trust me, I never want a repeat of that horrifying scenario."

CHAPTER 36

J had the shop to myself. Because of my early morning adventure with Dash, I had left Kingston at home, something I was regretting now. I could have used the support of a trusted buddy. I had paced the shop floor at least a dozen times, trying to organize the thoughts in my head.

I had invited Hazel to visit the shop so we could see each other before she left town. I decided not to bring up the new job or the embarrassing photo on Instagram. I didn't want to scare her off. I just wanted to gently nudge some information out of her. When my mind had finally settled on the possibility that Hazel had killed Jasper, I'd set right to work talking myself out of the hideous notion. Hazel was one of the sweetest people I knew. There just wasn't any way the woman who always met everyone early Monday morning with a smile and a box of donuts, donuts that she hand selected to make sure everyone had their favorite, had killed someone. Unfortunately, it seemed things had gone some-what awry for her in the time since I'd left the company. I was more than shocked to hear Jacob criticize her work. I wondered if the terrible picture had thrown her life into disarray more than I'd even considered.

I'd been so deep in thought, I hadn't seen Hazel walk past the window and was startled when the shop bell rang. She looked much cheerier than the last time I'd seen her, which helped ease some of the tension in my shoulders. She seemed like her old self.

"It's so much warmer today." She was still wearing the bright blue sweater. She pushed up the sleeves and held up her arm to display a big chunky, white and blue bracelet. "Look at this. I love that Mod Frock. And the owner is very knowledgeable and stylish. I told her she should pick up and move to the city with her shop."

I ignored the backhanded dig at our small town and walked over to show interest in her newest purchase. The sleeves of the sweater fell down again, and she brusquely pushed them back. In that second, all of the earlier tension returned. As Hazel shoved the fabric of the sweater back, I caught a scent, a very distinctive scent. It was Jacob's cologne.

Up until then, I'd had many links, but they hadn't formed a real chain until now.

"The bracelet goes nicely with the sweater." My voice sounded strained to my ears, but Hazel didn't seem to notice. "You look much happier than the last time I saw you," I noted. "What's changed?"

"We finally get to go back home. Lydia got word that we'd be given the green light to leave tomorrow." Hazel walked over to smell some of the flowers sitting around the shop. "Everyone except Jacob," she said. And then I heard it, the fake sympathy. I hadn't been looking for it before because I never, in a million years, would have thought the spry, smiling woman in front of me, who I'd shared hundreds of coffee breaks with, could be a cold-blooded murderer. Her flippant remark and the knowledge that she had not only killed Jasper but had framed Jacob for the crime boiled my blood just enough to start asking questions.

"I guess it's good that you're moving on to that new job. You can put this whole mess behind you."

Hazel breathed in the scent of a potted lavender plant. "That's true."

I walked to the shelf of potted herbs where she was standing and picked up a few of the dried leaves that had fallen off the plants. "I had a confusing conversation with Jacob this morning."

Hazel seemed more than surprised that I had talked to Jacob. "Oh?" Some of the breezy smile faded.

"He said you didn't get the job at Tremaine's. I just assumed you hadn't told him."

She hadn't let go of the stem of lavender yet, and the light purple stock pinched off between her fingers. "Yes, well no. It's none of his business," she said tersely. "It's no one's business. I'll be just as happy to never see any of them again." I'd unleashed someone who was far removed from the Hazel I knew. Her face tightened with anger as she spoke about her coworkers. "They are a snooty, selfish bunch of dimwits. Including Jacob. But I guess he won't have to worry about replacing me when he's behind bars for murder."

"You mean for the murder you committed?"

Her blue eyes bulged behind her glasses. "Never thought you would turn on me. I guess I even misjudged you." She turned, and I was sure she would rush from the store. But she took three steps and planted her face in her hands. Her shoulders shook. I walked to the work island to get her a tissue and reached it just as my phone buzzed with a new text.

I glanced at it. It was from Briggs. "Do you know where I can find Hazel Bancroft?"

I quickly sent back a reply. "Yes, she's in my shop, and you might want to hurry."

I walked over to Hazel. She grabbed the tissue from my hand and wiped her eyes but refused to look at me. "He was a cruel, awful person and he deserved to die." She stared out the front window as she spoke. "This whole last year I have lived with the humiliation of that picture. People snickering behind my back. Extra boxes of tissue on my desk. " She held up the one I'd given her. "I had to leave the company. Then Jacob—" She sobbed into the tissue. I felt genuinely bad for the woman. It was strange feeling so much empathy for a murderer, but I could feel her pain as she spoke. "I worked tirelessly for that man for years. The only thanks I got was a mediocre letter of recommendation."

My throat was dry from the shock of it all. "How long have you been planning this?"

She turned to me with a dark scowl. "I'd thought up so many scenarios of how I might take Jasper's life. I hated him that much. But when Jacob betrayed me, I decided to take them both. When the trip to Port Danby was planned, I knew my chance had come. And after I'd read that you had used your sense of smell to help the police solve murders—"

"You decided to frame Jacob by planting scented clues around the crime scene that would all lead back to one person."

A weak, sad laugh fell from her mouth. "You've still got a super nose. In my job, I learned a lot about people. I knew Jasper had an insomnia problem. He took a lot of naps in the day to make up for not sleeping at night, and he used sleeping pills, even for those naps. When the weather forecast showed rain, I knew everyone would just be lounging in their trailers waiting for the weather to clear. Jacob left for the morning, so I used that time to go into his trailer and put some of his cologne on my hands. The clove cigarette was a last second idea. I lit it and waved the smoke around to cover my clothes with the scent. Then I put it out and stuck it in an ashtray. When I saw Autumn leaving Jasper's trailer, I asked what Jasper was doing. She told me he was going to take a nap."

"One thing I don't understand," I said. "How did you know that Jacob would sleep walk right at the time of the murder?"

"That incriminating piece of evidence was a gift, a well timed coincidence. I didn't know—"

Her confession was interrupted when Detective Briggs raced into the shop looking as distraught as he'd been earlier in the day when he thought I was still on the plane. He saw me and the worry in his brow faded.

"Detective Briggs?" I made sure to say it as a question.

"Your text," he started. "Never mind." Without delay, he walked over to Hazel. "Hazel Bancroft, you are under arrest for the murder of Jasper Edmonton."

Officer Chinmoor lumbered into the shop with Hilda to finish the arrest.

Briggs saw me standing in the background watching the entire surreal event with shock. He joined me. "I'm sorry. I know she was a friend of yours."

"I still can't believe it. I have to hand it to her. She had things pretty well covered. Jacob's cologne, the clove cigarette."

Briggs nodded. "The DNA sample on the end of the clove cigarette was Hazel's. She lit the cigarette and picked up enough of the scent from the smoke to leave traces on the pillow. A pillow she knew would eventually pass by her friend with the million dollar nose."

I crossed my arms for comfort. "We were friends but she had no problem using me for her sordid scheme. I feel duped."

"No, she just had a good plan. She knew all her coworkers very well, it seems. Including all their habits."

"Hazel ran herself ragged making sure to take care of every-one's needs at Georgio's, and she was repaid with a cruel joke."

"Oh?"

"You need to check out Jasper Edmonton's Instagram account. And there are some other details I know that I'll explain later once the shock has worn off. It seems that this was pure and simple—a case of revenge."

CHAPTER 37

*E*lsie had not only saved herself from a Valentine's Day fiasco, she had turned her bakery date with Mr. Darcy into a triumph. Bright red and pink balloon bouquets floated up from the chairs and tables, and customers mingled with free caramel kiss cookies and tea while waiting for their turn to take a picture with the cardboard cutout.

Elsie spotted me on my way to my shop and slipped through her customers to hand me a free cookie. "Happy Valentine's Day, Pink, and thank you for keeping this day from complete chaos."

I glanced around at the happy faces. "Looks like everything turned out well then."

"It did. Turned out everyone was rather excited to take a picture with Mr. Darcy, even if he was made of cardboard. I've got my laptop open in the shop with the series playing. So some people are sitting inside watching Pride and Prejudice as they sip tea."

"Almost as good as being right there at Pemberley. Well, I better get into the shop. Ryder has some deliveries to make." I held up the cookie. "Thanks for the caramel kiss."

Ryder pulled on his coat as I stepped inside. "No Kingston today?"

"I figured there would just be too much going on to have to worry about him."

Ryder tapped a pile of mail on the counter. "Mail came early. Maggie said she got an extra early start today knowing people would be waiting for their Valentines. Which reminds me. Dash stopped by on his way to the marina." Ryder held up a rose made out of chocolate. "He was sorry he missed you."

I took the rose and out of habit brought it to my nose to smell, only to remember it was chocolate. "Hmm, almost better smelling than the real thing. So do you have everything you need?"

Ryder patted his coat pocket. "Delivery itinerary, keys and my phone if you need me."

"Perfect. And drive carefully."

Ryder walked out to the van. On big holidays, I rented a van for deliveries, but the store was profitable enough that I'd soon be buying a Pink's delivery van of our very own. I shuffled through the mail and found an envelope that I instantly recognized with Jacob's writing. It was a card with a pink rose on the front.

"Dear Lacey, Thanks for having my back last week. It seemed right from the start you knew I wasn't the suspect. That means a lot to me. Have a happy Valentine's Day and a wonderful future. You deserve both.
Love always, Jacob."

I SMILED as I pushed the card into the envelope. The week didn't turn out at all like I'd expected, but in the end, the right person was charged. It was hard not to feel as much anger as pity at poor Hazel.

The door to the shop opened, and Detective Briggs walked inside. My mind instantly shot to the possibility that he'd come in to buy flowers for someone. I was fretting about the notion when he walked up wearing a half smile. "Miss Pinkerton," he said with a polite nod.

"Detective Briggs."

He placed a small package hastily wrapped in pink tissue on the counter. "Happy Valentine's Day."

He'd come in not to buy another woman flowers but to bring me a gift. I nearly chortled in relief .

I picked up the package. "I wasn't expecting anything."

"I decided I needed to thank you for helping with the investigation . . . again."

"Even though I wasn't supposed to?"

"Even though you weren't supposed to." His brown eyes landed on the package in my hand. "It's nothing much. Just thought it might come in handy."

I laughed as I pulled open the tissue. "So you're a practical gift kind of guy." The tissue fell away revealing a notebook and pen identical to the ones he used.

"For future investigations," he said quietly.

"I love it." The moments where we gazed at each other without any emotions except admiration had grown longer and more frequent. And I might have been imagining it, but they felt just a touch more intense each time too. "Thank you, Detective Briggs."

"You're welcome, Miss Pinkerton."

Firefly Junction

Did Lola's mysterious ghostly photos pique your interest? You can read more about the Cider Ridge Inn and its cocky, irritating and far too appealing ghost in *Death in the Park* the first book in my new cozy mystery series, **Firefly Junction.**

Release Date: February 18, 2018

Tulips are blooming and spring is in the air in Port Danby. Lacey 'Pink' Pinkerton, the local flower shop owner and occasional detective's assistant, is once again called upon to help sniff out the clues in a murder investigation. **Full blurb coming soon.**

Release Date: March 18, 2018

CARAMEL KISSES

View recipe online: www.londonlovett.com/caramel-kisses

Caramel
KISSES

Ingredients:

1 cup butter (melted)
3/4 cup brown sugar
1 tsp vanilla
1 1/2 cups finely chopped pecans
11oz candy caramels
2 1/4 cups all-purpose flour
1/2 tsp baking powder

Directions:

1. Pre-heat oven to 350°.

2. Mix together flour and baking powder, set aside.

3. Melt 1 cup butter.

4. Stir 3/4 cup brown sugar into the melted butter. Add 1/2 cup chopped pecans.

5. Stir dry ingredients, flour and baking powder, into the wet mixture until well mixed.

6. Roll about 1 1/2 tablespoons of dough into a ball then shape by pinching the top and flattening the bottom to resemble a chocolate kiss candy.

7. Place on baking sheet.

8. Bake at 350° for 12-14 minutes.

9. Let kisses cool completely.

10. Melt the candy caramels with 1/4 cup water in a double boiler or microwave.

11. Put remaining chopped pecans in a small bowl.

12. Dip flat end of the cooled cookie in melted caramel and then immediately into chopped pecans to coat.

13. Place dipped cookie on wax or parchment paper and wait for caramel to set.

14. ENJOY!

ABOUT THE AUTHOR

London Lovett is the author of the Port Danby Cozy Mystery series and the new Firefly Junction Cozy Mystery series.. She loves getting caught up in a good mystery and baking delicious new treats!

Subscribe to London's newsletter to never miss an update.

https://www.londonlovett.com/
londonlovettwrites@gmail.com

CPSIA information can be obtained
at www.ICGtesting.com
Printed in the USA
LVHW091257240222
711924LV00011B/128

9 781983 903090